BRANCH

DATE DUE

To Every Season

A FAMILY HOLIDAY COOKBOOK

To Every Season

A FAMILY HOLIDAY COOKBOOK

∾ WRITTEN AND ILLUSTRATED BY ∾

JANE BRESKIN ZALBEN

SIMON & SCHUSTER BOOKS FOR YOUNG READERS

I wish to thank my publishing "family"—Stephanie Owens Lurie, Michele Coppola, Paul Zakris, and the staff of Simon & Schuster Books for Young Readers—for their patience, creativity, and support, and my own family—Steven, Alexander, and Jonathan—for their love and appreciation of my "culinary" efforts over the years.

—J.B.Z.

SIMON & SCHUSTER BOOKS FOR YOUNG READERS
An imprint of Simon & Schuster Children's Publishing Division
1230 Avenue of the Americas, New York, New York 10020
Copyright © 1999 by Jane Breskin Zalben
SIMON & SCHUSTER BOOKS FOR YOUNG READERS
is a trademark of Simon & Schuster.
Book design by Jane Breskin Zalben
The text of this book is set in 12-point Bembo.
The illustrations are rendered in watercolor with a triple zero brush.
The borders on pages 38-39 are adapted from an
eighteenth-century Sephardic textile.
Jacket border fabric design used with permission of the
Victoria and Albert Museum/William Morris Collection by Rose & Hubble
Printed in the United States of America
10 9 8 7 6 5 4 3 2 1

LIBRARY OF CONGRESS CATALOGING-IN-PUBLICATION DATA
Zalben, Jane Breskin.
To every season : a family holiday cookbook / recipes, text,
and art by Jane Breskin Zalben.—1st ed.
p. cm.
Summary: Gives brief histories and recipes for such holidays as
Valentine's Day, Easter, Passover, Independence Day, and Kwanzaa.
ISBN 0-689-81797-5
1. Holiday cookery—Juvenile literature. 2. Holidays—Juvenile literature.
[1. Holiday cookery. 2. Holidays. 3. Cookery.] I. Title.
TX739.Z35 1999
641.5'68—dc21
98-35393
CIP   AC

To every thing there is a season,
and a time to every purpose under the heaven.
ECCLESIASTES, CHAPTER 3, VERSE 1

And also that every man should eat and drink,
and enjoy the good of all his labour, it is the gift of God.
ECCLESIASTES, CHAPTER 3, VERSE 13

AUTHOR'S NOTE

*H*olidays bring families and friends together to share special times, special traditions, and special foods. This is a cookbook for the whole family, with recipes that can be made and enjoyed by adults and children for holidays throughout the year. When children work alongside adults to help prepare these special dishes, cooking becomes fun. By sharing love, family histories, and dreams while we cook, we turn an ordinary task into something meaningful. Cooking is a way for generations to connect: It is a time to talk, to teach customs and values, to allow children to take chances, and to get close. It is also a way to give children a sense of accomplishment: They do math when they measure; they see things rise and fall through the science of chemistry; they create art by cutting a cookie shape or decorating a cupcake. And nothing can top the moment when a special treat comes to the table, the child says, "I made it!" and everyone sighs, "Ooh," and "Aah."

Although this book is organized by the calendar year, the recipes are interchangeable for the winter, spring, summer, and fall seasons. Some dishes are traditionally associated with a specific holiday, of course, but you should feel free to swap from one section to another, or use recipes for holidays your family doesn't celebrate.

Effort has been made to allow for different dietary needs. For instance, if you keep kosher, you can still make corned beef and cabbage or plum pudding: All of the recipes in this book are kosher. If you make substitutions, such as margarine for butter, recipes become pareve (made without milk or meat). Recipes are also halal (without pork or alcohol); individuals should follow their own religious guidelines and make substitutions accordingly. In addition, there are many recipes for vegetarians.

Within each family, adults should decide which tasks are suitable for the individual child. Some kitchen equipment, such as knives, graters, scissors, beaters, mixers, food processors, ovens, and stoves, should only be used with adult supervision. Oven mitts, pot holders, and aprons should be used each time you cook.

To everyone in every season who uses this family cookbook, good health and happy holidays,

Jane Breskin Zalben

CONTENTS

NEW YEAR'S DAY • *10*

Jack Frost's Tropical Punch • *12*

Potato Crescent Horns • *12*

Three-Bean Chili and Guacamole • *14*

Quarterback Quiche • *15*

VALENTINE'S DAY • *16*

Heart-Shaped Sugar Cookies • *18*

Chocolate-Lover's Lollipops • *19*

Cupid Cupcakes with Pink Frosting • *20*

ST. PATRICK'S DAY • *22*

Lucky Clover Salad • *24*

Irish Soda Bread • *25*

Molly's Potato and Barley Soup • *26*

Corned Beef and Cabbage • *27*

APRIL FOOLS' DAY • *28*

Oatmeal Raisin "Ant" Cookies • *30*

Lemon Poppy Pound Cake • *31*

EASTER • *32*

Decorating Easter Eggs • *34*

E. Bunny's Chopped Egg Salad • *35*

Hot Cross Breakfast Buns • *36*

Sunday Roast Lamb • *37*

PASSOVER • *38*

The Seder Plate • *40*

Apple-and-Walnut Ḥaroset • *42*

Date-and-Almond Ḥaroset • *42*

Vegetarian Matzoh Ball Soup • *43*

Classic Brisket • *44*

Fanny's Flourless Chocolate Cake • *45*

MOTHER'S DAY • *46*

Fluffy Cinnamon French Toast • *48*

Mama's Mocha Truffles • *48*

Chocolate-Dipped Strawberries • *49*

MEMORIAL DAY • *50*

Waldorf Salad • *52*

Cucumber, Yogurt and Mint Salad • *52*

Orange Couscous • *53*

Wild Rice Pilaf • *53*

Sweet and Sour Meatballs • *54*

Veteran's Vegetable Kebabs • *55*

FATHER'S DAY • *56*

Belgian Waffles and Blueberry Pancakes • *58*

Chocolate Chip Cookies • *59*

Papa's Lemonade • *59*

INDEPENDENCE DAY • *60*

Firecracker Potato Salad • *62*

Stars and Stripes Fusilli • *63*

Patriotic Cheesecake • *64*

All-American Fruit Salad • *65*

LABOR DAY • *66*

Laid-Back Banana Bread • *68*

Easy Chicken Salad • *69*

Virtual Burgers • *70*

Old-Fashioned Peach Cobbler • *71*

September S'mores • *71*

HALLOWEEN • *72*

Halloween Haunted House Party Foods • *73*

Acorn Squash Soup • *74*

Black and Orange Pasta • *75*

Monster Muffins • *76*

Pumpkin Cookies • *77*

THANKSGIVING • *78*

Cranberry Orange Relish • *80*

Chestnut Stuffing • *81*

Roast Turkey with Potatoes and Carrots • *82*

Mushroom Gravy • *83*

Pilgrim Pumpkin Pie • *84*

CHANUKAH • *86*

Pearl's Potato Latkes • *88*

Avi's Cinnamon-Stick Applesauce • *89*

Bubbe's Baked Apples • *89*

Uncle Solly's Sufganiyot/Jelly Doughnuts • *90*

KWANZAA • *92*

Buttermilk Corn Bread • *94*

Sweet Potato Pudding • *95*

Baked Chicken Nuggets • *96*

Black-Eyed Pea Cutlets and Collard Greens • *97*

CHRISTMAS • *98*

Santa's Elves' Eggless Eggnog • *100*

Mulled Apple Cider • *101*

Candy Cane Hot Chocolate • *102*

Spiced and Iced Gingerbread Animals • *103*

Yuletide Date Logs and Snowballs • *104*

Christmas Cranberry-Apple Tea Loaf • *105*

Mrs. Claus's Plum Pudding • *106*

GLOSSARY • *108*

INDEX • *110*

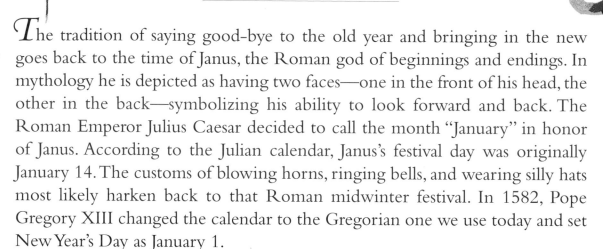

NEW YEAR'S DAY

*T*he tradition of saying good-bye to the old year and bringing in the new goes back to the time of Janus, the Roman god of beginnings and endings. In mythology he is depicted as having two faces—one in the front of his head, the other in the back—symbolizing his ability to look forward and back. The Roman Emperor Julius Caesar decided to call the month "January" in honor of Janus. According to the Julian calendar, Janus's festival day was originally January 14. The customs of blowing horns, ringing bells, and wearing silly hats most likely harken back to that Roman midwinter festival. In 1582, Pope Gregory XIII changed the calendar to the Gregorian one we use today and set New Year's Day as January 1.

Different cultures celebrate New Year's at different times of the year. Some Native American tribes celebrate a "New Year's Jubilee" on the day of the first full moon in February. The Jewish New Year, called "Rosh Hashanah," begins on the first day of Tishri, the first month of the Jewish calendar, which usually corresponds with September in the Gregorian calendar. The sound of a shofar, a ram's horn, ushers in the year. The Islamic New Year, "Ras al-Sana," is marked with quiet worship on the first day of the Islamic month of Muharram. Like Native Americans, Jews, and Muslims, the Chinese celebrate New Year's according to the lunar calendar. Sometime between January and February parades are staged with people in elaborate dragon costumes, firecrackers are set off, and feasts are held. One custom common to different cultural New Year's celebrations is to make resolutions to start the year afresh with a clean slate.

It is fun to stay up until midnight at a New Year's Eve party on December 31 and toast your friends and family with a festive punch. Or you may prefer a celebration over brunch on New Year's Day.

NEW YEAR'S DAY

Jack Frost's Tropical Punch
Potato Crescent Horns
Three-Bean Chili and Guacamole
Quarterback Quiche

Jack Frost's Tropical Punch

Our family drinks this punch year-round—winter, summer, you name it!

1 liter seltzer or club soda

48 ounces cranberry juice

2 quarts grapefruit juice

1 fresh lime, for squeezing

2 fresh limes, thinly sliced

About 24 fresh raspberries

2–3 trays of ice cubes

1. Into a large punch bowl, combine seltzer, and cranberry and grapefruit juices.
2. Squeeze fresh lime and add juice to bowl. Add sliced limes and raspberries to float on top. (Can substitute sliced lemons and strawberries.)
3. Add 2–3 trays of ice cubes.

Yield: Serves 12–14 (depending on how thirsty the crowd is).

Potato Crescent Horns

I created this recipe for the Hicksville (Long Island) Library's celebration of the 350th anniversary of the potato by "marrying" two of my favorite dishes: rugelach pastry (crescent cookies) and potato knishes. These crescent-shaped rolls remind me of New Year's Eve party horns.

Filling

1 small onion, peeled and diced

6 garlic cloves, peeled and minced, or ½ teaspoon garlic powder

Vegetable oil for sautéing

4 large baking potatoes

½ cup low-fat milk

Salt and pepper to taste

Dough

3 large eggs (reserve 1 yolk)

1 tablespoon apple cider vinegar

½ cup vegetable oil

½ cup low-fat milk

5–6 cups unbleached flour, sifted

2 teaspoons baking powder

¼ teaspoon salt

1 cup water, room temperature

1 teaspoon cold water

Extra flour

1. *Filling*: Sauté diced onion and, if desired, fresh minced garlic cloves in oil, over low flame, 10 minutes or until translucent. Set frying pan aside. (If powdered garlic is used, add to potatoes at step 3.)

2. Boil baking potatoes about an hour until they are soft. (Pierce a skewer through the center to see if they're done.) Drain. Cool 5 minutes in cold water. Peel. Rinse. Place in large mixing bowl.

3. Mash potatoes by hand or with a mixer, adding milk, salt, pepper, and garlic powder (see step 1). Mix in sautéed onions.

4. Preheat oven to 375°.

5. *Dough*: Separate 1 egg. (Reserve the yolk for glaze later in the recipe.) In a separate mixing bowl, beat remaining egg white with other 2 eggs. Add apple cider vinegar, oil, and milk.

6. Sift together flour, baking powder, and salt in another bowl. Gradually stir into wet mixture. Then slowly add water until consistency is elastic.

7. Dust fingers and pastry board with flour. Knead dough in bowl until smooth. Remove from bowl and divide dough into 2 balls.

8. Roll 1 ball at a time on floured surface with a rolling pin. Form a 9-by-20-inch rectangle. With a rubber spatula, cover rectangle with thin layer of potato filling. Cut triangles so that they have a 2-inch base (see diagram). Beginning at the base, tightly roll dough up to the point. (This is the part that reminds me of a New Year's Eve party horn.) Place each crescent, point down, on a parchment-lined or nonstick cookie sheet.

9. Using a fork, stir together reserved yolk and 1 teaspoon cold water to make a glaze. With a pastry brush, paint each roll with the glaze. Bake 30–40 minutes or until light brown.

Yield: 3 dozen.

Note: Other fillings you can add to the potato layer before rolling and baking the horn: a raw cocktail frankfurter, some chopped spinach and broccoli, sautéed mushrooms, or shredded cheese to taste.

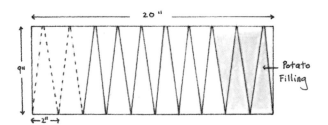

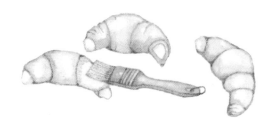

Three-Bean Chili and Guacamole

1 cup black beans, canned or dried
1 cup red kidney beans, canned or dried
1 cup pinto beans, canned or dried
3 cups water
4 plum tomatoes, whole
1 cup tomato sauce
1 teaspoon soy sauce
1 tablespoon grape jelly

8 garlic cloves, peeled and minced
1 large sweet red pepper, chopped
1 medium onion, peeled and diced
1 large carrot, peeled and cut into ½-inch slices
1 large celery stalk, cut into ½-inch slices
1 teaspoon oregano
½ teaspoon ground cumin
¼ teaspoon red pepper flakes

1. If you use dried beans, soak them in water overnight until they swell (2 cups of water to every cup of beans).

2. In an 8-quart pot, add beans, 3 cups water, plum tomatoes, tomato and soy sauces, and grape jelly. Add garlic, red pepper, onion, carrot, celery, and spices.

3. Cover pot. Simmer over medium flame 2 hours or until beans are tender. Serve immediately, or refrigerate and reheat.

4. Serve with tortillas, chips, cooked rice, or corn, or stuff mixture inside a burrito or taco shell. Garnish with shredded cheese of your choice (cheddar, Monterey Jack), freshly diced onion, chopped pitted black olives, sour cream, or guacamole. All garnishes are optional.

5. *Guacamole*: Peel and pit one large ripe avocado. Mash with a fork in bowl, leaving small chunks. Add 1 teaspoon lemon juice, a pinch of red cayenne pepper, and 2 tablespoons diced tomatoes or tomatillos. Mix. Always serve guacamole immediately, or it turns color.

Yield: Serves 12.

Quarterback Quiche

For New Year's Day brunch or during the football game.

Crust

6 tablespoons margarine, softened
8 ounces cream cheese, softened
½ teaspoon vanilla extract
1½ cups unbleached flour, sifted
Dash of nutmeg or mace
Pinch of orange zest
Pinch of salt
Extra flour

Filling

Vegetable or olive oil for sautéing
4 garlic cloves, peeled and minced
1 plum tomato, diced
½ medium-size zucchini, chopped
¾ cup broccoli or spinach, chopped
2 large eggs, beaten
1 cup low-fat milk
1 teaspoon nutmeg
Shredded cheese of your choice

1. Preheat oven to 350°.
2. *Crust*: With an electric mixer, cream margarine, cream cheese, and vanilla. Add flour, nutmeg or mace, orange zest, and salt. Knead dough into a ball. On a flour-dusted surface, use a rolling pin to roll dough into a circle large enough to fit into a large pie or quiche pan. Press circle of dough into pan. Pinch around the perimeter with thumb and forefinger to make a pretty scalloped edge.
3. Place a 9-inch cake pan on dough to prevent crust from shrinking, and bake in oven 5–7 minutes until lightly browned. Remove from oven.
4. *Filling*: In a large frying pan coated with oil, sauté garlic for several minutes until tender, then vegetables, over medium heat for about 5 minutes. Scatter onto crust.
5. In a mixing bowl beat eggs, milk, and nutmeg. Pour into quiche pan. Bake 1 hour. Five minutes before the end of baking time, sprinkle cheese on top of quiche and continue to bake. Serve with a tossed salad.

Yield: 1 large quiche.

VALENTINE'S DAY

The Romans celebrated the feast of Lupercalia on February 15, in honor of the god Lupercus, who protected them from wolves. During the festivities, a young man would draw a girl's name out of a bowl to be his partner in games and dances. The girl whose name the boy drew would be his sweetheart for a year.

After Constantine declared Christianity the official religion of Rome in the fourth century C.E., the Romans could no longer honor their pagan god Lupercus. Instead they began celebrating St. Valentine, a priest beheaded by the Roman Emperor Claudius II on February 14. The emperor forbade his soldiers to marry, because he thought they wouldn't want to leave their families to go to war. Valentine believed in love, however, and was put to death for performing marriage ceremonies. He became the patron saint of lovers.

Today, in the spirit of the holiday, we exchange pretty cards in red with white lace, decorated with hearts, cherubs, and Cupid—all symbols of romance. Cupid comes from the ancient Greek myth of Eros (Romans renamed him Cupid), the son of Aphrodite, the goddess of love and beauty. He wields a bow so he can pierce his human targets with love arrows.

VALENTINE'S DAY

Heart-Shaped Sugar Cookies
Chocolate-Lover's Lollipops
Cupid Cupcakes with Pink Frosting

Heart-Shaped Sugar Cookies

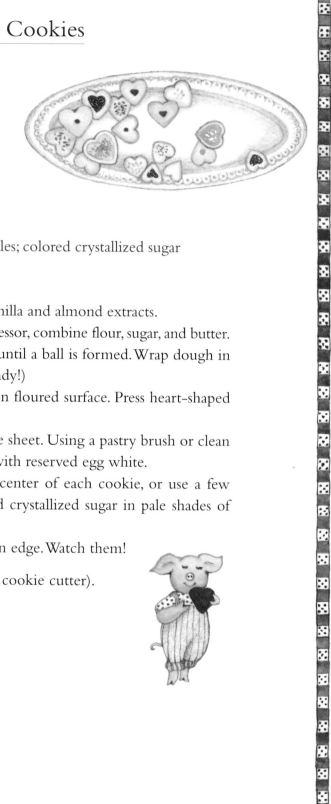

1 large egg, separated
2 tablespoons orange juice
1 teaspoon vanilla extract
½ teaspoon almond extract (optional)
3 cups unbleached flour, sifted
1 cup granulated sugar
1 cup unsalted butter, softened
Extra flour
Decorations: Red Hots; pink, white, and red sprinkles; colored crystallized sugar

1. Preheat oven to 350°.
2. In a small bowl, beat egg yolk, orange juice, and vanilla and almond extracts.
3. In a large bowl, using an electric mixer or food processor, combine flour, sugar, and butter. Add egg mixture, and mix together. Knead dough until a ball is formed. Wrap dough in wax paper. Refrigerate 1 hour. (Get decorations ready!)
4. With a rolling pin, roll dough, as thin as possible, on floured surface. Press heart-shaped cookie cutter in dough.
5. Put cookies on nonstick or parchment-lined cookie sheet. Using a pastry brush or clean 1-inch-wide paintbrush, glaze top of each cookie with reserved egg white.
6. *Decorations*: Place a Red Hots cinnamon heart in center of each cookie, or use a few pink, white, and red sprinkles or a dash of colored crystallized sugar in pale shades of pink and red.
7. Bake 10 minutes until cookies have a slightly golden edge. Watch them!

Yield: 6 dozen (varies according to the size of your cookie cutter).

Chocolate-Lover's Lollipops

Inexpensive plastic molds can be bought at cooking stores or specialty candy shops. Use white, milk, semisweet, or bittersweet chocolate.

1 pound chocolate (or more if you want)
Plastic lollipop molds, lollipop sticks, paintbrush, and wax paper

1. Melt chocolate in double boiler on top of stove. (If you don't have a double boiler, put chocolate in one saucepan inside a slightly larger one filled halfway with water, making sure water does not get into chocolate.) When water boils, remove from flame. Stir until chocolate is melted. (Or melt in a glass bowl in a microwave oven, at low power, about 4 minutes for every pound of chocolate. Stir for smoothness.)
2. Pour some chocolate into a cup. With a small paintbrush, coat inside of mold with chocolate to prevent bubbles and ensure a smooth surface. Hold mold up to light to make sure every crevice is painted.
3. Spoon melted chocolate into individual molds. Put lollipop stick in groove of mold, halfway up.
4. Place in refrigerator for about 10 minutes until hard.
5. Turn mold over, holding close to a tabletop, and carefully press plastic side of mold to pop out chocolate lollipops onto wax paper.
6. Wrap individually or bunch several together with cellophane or plastic wrap, and tie with a pretty ribbon. Give "bouquet" to your Valentine.

Yield: 1 dozen (depending on size of mold).

Cupid Cupcakes

Cupcakes are the perfect treat for anyone's "honey." Serve to your sweetheart plain or decorate the top of each cupcake with pale pink vanilla frosting.

3 cups unbleached flour, sifted	1 cup strong coffee
1 teaspoon baking soda	1 teaspoon maple syrup
1 teaspoon baking powder	1 teaspoon molasses (optional)
3 large eggs, separated	1 teaspoon ginger
1 cup granulated sugar	1 teaspoon cinnamon
¼ cup vegetable oil	1 teaspoon allspice
Juice of one lemon	1 tablespoon finely ground almonds
1 cup honey	1 teaspoon cream of tartar

2 dozen 2½-inch silver-colored paper cupcake liners

1. Preheat oven to 350°.
2. Sift flour, baking soda, and baking powder into large bowl. Set aside.
3. In another large bowl, with an electric mixer, beat egg yolks and sugar until foamy. Add oil, lemon juice, honey, coffee, maple syrup, and molasses. Add spices. Mix.
4. Combine wet ingredients with dry ingredients.
5. Grind whole almonds in electric blender. Set aside.
6. In a separate bowl, beat egg whites with cream of tartar until stiff peaks form. (Make sure beaters are clean, or peaks won't form!) Using a spatula, gently fold egg whites and almonds into batter.
7. Line 2 muffin tins with paper cupcake liners, preferably silver. Pour batter ⅔ full to allow cupcakes to double in height.
8. Bake 30 minutes. Cool muffin tins on a rack ½ hour. Remove from tins and frost cupcakes.

Yield: 2 dozen.

Pink Frosting

This vanilla frosting is ideal with the honey cupcakes. A touch of red food coloring makes it look fairylike and magical, as though Cupid made it himself!

8 ounces cream cheese, softened
½ cup unsalted butter, softened
1 pound confectioners' sugar, sifted
2 teaspoons vanilla extract
8 drops of red food coloring (or beet juice)
½ cup dark or light raisins
½ cup sweet pecans, toasted and chopped

Decorations

Pink, red, or white jelly beans
White sprinkles
Red Hots
White-chocolate mini-morsels

1. In a large bowl, blend cream cheese and butter with electric mixer. Add sugar, vanilla, and food coloring until blended to a pink color.
2. Continue to mix, adding raisins and pecans.
3. Smooth frosting over cupcakes with spatula.
4. Decorate top of each cupcake with one pink, red, or white jelly bean, some white sprinkles, a Red Hots cinnamon heart, or a few white-chocolate mini-morsels.

ST. PATRICK'S DAY

St. Patrick, or Maewyn, as he was originally called, is the patron saint of Ireland. He was born around 389 C.E. in Britannia, the ancient name for Britain, Wales, and Scotland. At the age of sixteen he was forced to work as a herdsman when Irish plunderers raided his village. During his time of servitude he prayed and found his "calling." Six years later he escaped and went to a monastery to study religion under St. Germain, a bishop in Gaul. He stayed for over a decade. In 431 the Roman pope sent Palladius, another bishop, to Ireland. This disappointed Maewyn. When Palladius failed in his mission, Maewyn was appointed as the second bishop. Upon his return to Ireland in 432, he officially adopted the Christian name Patrick. He traveled throughout Ireland, setting up monasteries, churches, and schools to convert the Irish country folk to Christianity. Though his efforts upset the Celtic Druids, an order of priests, wizards, magicians, and soothsayers who advised chiefs in ancient Ireland, his lifetime goal of conversion was successful. The Catholic Church later made him a saint. St. Patrick's Day is celebrated on March 17 because he died on March 17, 461.

According to Irish folklore, St. Patrick delivered a sermon that drove all the snakes out of Ireland. To this day there isn't a snake in the entire country!

The anniversary of his death is celebrated with parades, traditional feasts, jigs, and songs. Many people wear a shamrock—a three-leaf clover representing the Trinity: the Father, the Son, and the Holy Spirit—which has become the national symbol of Ireland. St. Patrick's Day came to Boston, a popular settling place for Irish immigrants, in 1737, and from there spread across America. On this day, whether people are Irish or not, they often wear something green, the color of the "Emerald Isle," to share in the festivities of this merry holiday.

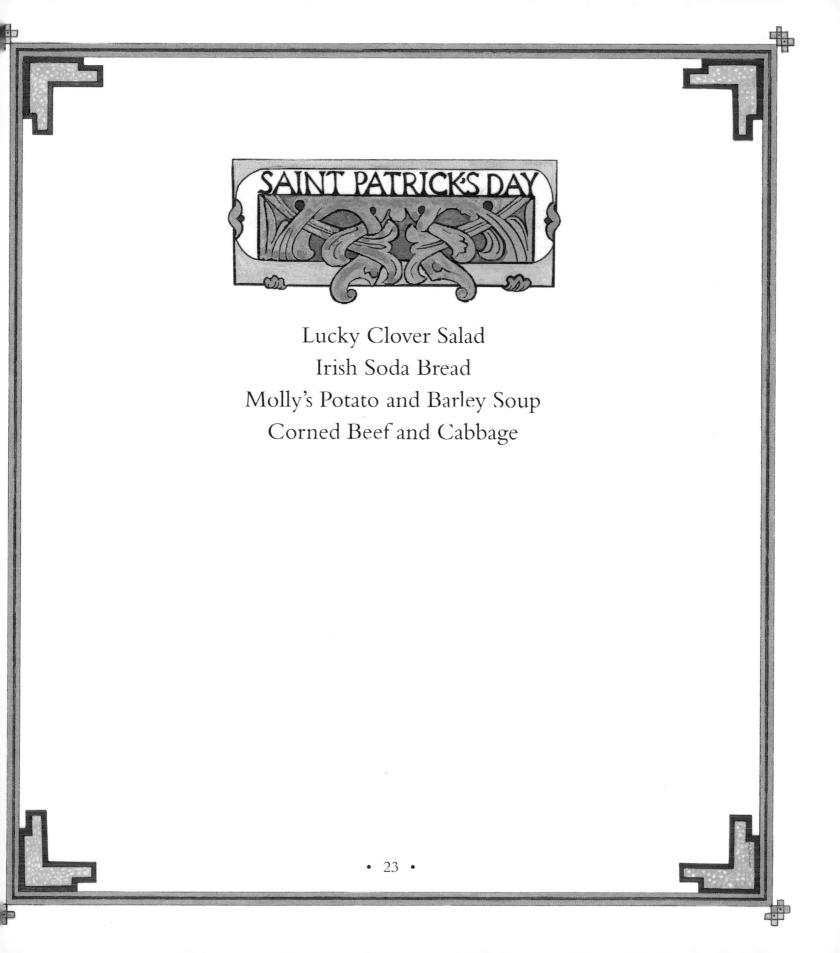

SAINT PATRICK'S DAY

Lucky Clover Salad

Irish Soda Bread

Molly's Potato and Barley Soup

Corned Beef and Cabbage

Lucky Clover Salad

Alfalfa sprouts combined with clover can be found in the vegetable section of supermarkets. This is an easy alternative to searching the front lawn for clover. However, if you happen to find one with four leaves, definitely add it to the recipe—it might bring you good luck! Everything in this salad is green.

Salad	Dressing
1 head of Boston lettuce	¼ cup olive oil
Large handful of spinach leaves	2 teaspoons fresh lemon or lime juice
½ cup watercress	¼ cup balsamic vinegar
1 cucumber, peeled and thinly sliced	¼ cup fresh basil, chopped
3½ ounces mixed clover/alfalfa sprouts	
6–8 pitted green olives	
6 small green bell peppers	

1. *Salad*: Wash lettuce, spinach, and watercress. Pat dry with paper towels. Cut into bite-size pieces. Put into large bowl.
2. Add cucumber slices. Gently mix in clover/alfalfa sprouts. Scatter olives.
3. *Dressing*: In a separate bowl, mix olive oil, lemon or lime juice, and vinegar, using a wire whisk. Add basil. Continue to stir. Pour over salad. Toss gently.
4. Arrange salad on plates. Decorate each plate with the sliced-off bottom of a green pepper—it looks like a shamrock!

Yield: Serves 6.

Pot of Gold

Irish Soda Bread

There is something so soothing about family and friends sitting down together to enjoy tea and warm soda bread.

2 cups unbleached flour

2 teaspoons baking soda

2 teaspoons baking powder

½ teaspoon salt

1 tablespoon granulated sugar

2 tablespoons unsalted butter, softened

1 cup buttermilk

½ cup light raisins

½ cup dark raisins

1 tablespoon caraway seeds

Extra flour

Milk for coating bread

1. Preheat oven to 375°.
2. In a large bowl, sift together flour, baking soda, and baking powder. Add salt and sugar.
3. In an electric mixer or food processor, blend butter with the dry ingredients until mixture is mealy. While mixing, gradually pour in buttermilk to form dough. Mix in raisins and caraway seeds.
4. Dust fingers with flour. Knead dough into round 2-inch-high loaf.
5. Put loaf on greased or parchment-lined cookie sheet. Using pastry brush or a clean 1-inch-wide paintbrush, coat loaf with milk until surface is smooth. With a sharp knife, make a ½-inch-deep slit both ways to form a cross on top of loaf to prevent bread from cracking while it bakes. Sprinkle flour on top of cross.
6. Bake 35 minutes until light brown. Serve unsliced on plate to display flour-dusted cross on top of crust.

Yield: 1 loaf.

Molly's Potato and Barley Soup

This hearty winter soup is perfect for a frosty day in March. Potatoes are found in many Irish stews and soups. The Irish white potato was brought to the shores of Ireland from the wrecks of Spanish explorers in 1588. Ireland was the first European country to grow the potato. The people found the vegetable easy to grow, tasty, and filling—good for feeding many mouths in large families. In 1719, Irish immigrants introduced the potato to America, where it became an important crop.

½ cup dried lima beans or 1 cup frozen lima beans
8–10 cups water (start with 8 cups; add more as you're cooking)
1 large carrot, peeled and cut into ½-inch slices
1 large celery stalk with leaves, chopped
5–7 medium mushrooms, sliced
3 large potatoes, peeled and cut into chunks
2 cups barley
½ pound beef chuck or lamb, cut
   into 1-inch cubes (optional)
1 teaspoon soy sauce or Worcestershire sauce
Salt and pepper to taste
1 cup fresh dill, chopped (reserve 10 small sprigs)

1. Soak dried lima beans in 1 cup water overnight in a small bowl. By morning, they will swell to 1 cup. Or use 1 cup frozen lima beans.
2. Fill a large pot with water. Add beans, vegetables, barley, and beef chuck or lamb (omit meat for vegetarian soup).
3. Add soy or Worcestershire sauce, salt and pepper, and dill.
4. Simmer in covered pot for 2 hours or until barley is soft.
5. Serve each portion piping hot with sprig of the feathery green dill.

Yield: Serves 10.

Corned Beef and Cabbage

Corned beef and cabbage is a traditional dish enjoyed by many Irish-Americans. Corned beef is usually sold in a pouch, already pickled. If corned beef isn't available in your supermarket, you can create your own brine by soaking beef brisket in a mixture of salt water and pickling spices a week before cooking. For the brine use 1 cup of salt for every quart of water. Pickling spice can be bought already mixed. It is made up of cinnamon, allspice, mustard seed, coriander, bay leaves, ginger, chili peppers, black pepper, cloves, mace, and cardamom. In the refrigerator, turn meat twice a day, coating in salty brine and spices for about a week.

Brine to cure meat

1 tablespoon kosher salt
1½ ounces mixed pickling spices
Water to cover meat

For cooking

4 pounds beef brisket soaked in brine,
 or pre-pickled beef
10 cups water
1 medium cabbage, quartered
16–24 tiny new or red potatoes

1. Remove pickled beef from plastic pouch (or add homemade pickled beef, pouring off any brine) and place it in an 8-quart covered pot filled with 10 cups of water. Simmer over low flame for 3–4 hours until tender.
2. Twenty minutes before the end of cooking time, add quartered cabbage and potatoes.
3. Slice steaming meat against the grain, about ½ inch thick, using a sharp knife on a wooden cutting board. Serve with hunks of pumpernickel bread.

Yield: Serves 8 hefty eaters.

APRIL FOOLS' DAY

Some think that April Fools' Day began in France in the late sixteenth century. Up until then the French had celebrated New Year's Day on the first day of spring. When King Charles IX adopted the Gregorian calendar, which began the year on January 1, many forgot the new date. They were therefore called "poisson d'Avril," or "April Fish," because young fish are easy to trick and hook. The French began sending silly little presents to one another on the first of April. Another explanation is that April Fools' Day originated out of "Holi," a Hindu festival for spring celebrated in India. In Scotland, the "Hunting of the Gowk" (gowk is a cuckoo bird—one to be fooled) was practiced on April 1. In England, April 1 was called "All Fools' Day." On April 1, 1860, a fictitious holiday was publicized with invitations to the Tower of London to view the "Annual Ceremony of Washing the White Lions." When the American colonies formed, settlers brought their European customs with them. Since then, on April 1 we play harmless practical jokes and shout, "April Fool!"

My favorite prank as a child was to put an ice cube with a tiny rubber bug in the center into my father's orange juice. To make your own, buy small plastic bugs and insert one in each section of an ice-cube tray. Add water and freeze. Then add to your victim's drink and watch him or her "bug out"!

APRIL FOOLS' DAY

Oatmeal Raisin "Ant" Cookies
Lemon Poppy Pound Cake

Oatmeal Raisin "Ant" Cookies

Pretend the raisins in this recipe are large ants. (There are people who actually eat chocolate-covered ants as well as crickets, worms, grasshoppers, beetles, and other insects!) For variety, mix ½ cup dark and ½ cup light raisins. They might be less crunchy than your local insect, but I'd rather go with the raisins. If you like crunchiness, add chopped walnuts!

1 cup butter, softened
1 cup brown sugar
½ cup granulated sugar
2 large eggs, beaten
1 teaspoon vanilla extract
1 teaspoon maple syrup
1½ cups unbleached flour, sifted

1 teaspoon baking soda
1 teaspoon cinnamon
Pinch of salt (optional)
3 cups uncooked oats
1 cup raisins
½ cup chopped walnuts

1. Preheat oven to 350°.
2. Cream butter and both sugars with an electric mixer. Add eggs, vanilla, and maple syrup into mixture.
3. In another bowl, combine flour, baking soda, cinnamon, and salt. Add to batter mixture. Stir in oats, raisins, and walnuts.
4. Line cookie sheets with parchment baking paper. Drop a tablespoon of batter for each cookie, about 1 dozen drops on each cookie sheet.
5. Bake about 15 minutes or until the edges are a light golden brown.
6. Cool 2 minutes on a rack. Place on dessert plate or in cookie jar.

Yield: 4 dozen.

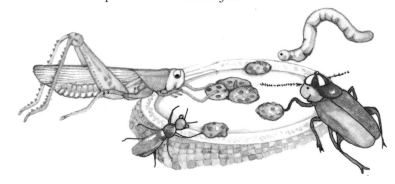

Lemon Poppy Pound Cake

Tell everyone you put the finest, tiniest, most perfectly round mites in this scrumptious lemony cake. Okay, so they're poppy seeds.

1½ cups butter, softened

2½–3 cups granulated sugar

4 large eggs, beaten

2 teaspoons vanilla extract

1 teaspoon lemon extract

1 cup sour cream

⅓ cup freshly squeezed lemon juice
  (also add 1–2 tablespoons of pulp)

Rinds of 2 medium-size lemons, grated

4 cups unbleached flour, sifted

1 tablespoon baking powder

½ teaspoon salt

2 teaspoons poppy seeds

Optional toppings

Whipped cream

Lemon zest

Extra poppy seeds

1. Preheat oven to 350°.
2. In large bowl, cream butter and sugar with an electric mixer.
   Add eggs, vanilla and lemon extracts, sour cream, lemon juice, pulp left over from the lemon, and grated lemon rind.
3. In a separate bowl, sift together flour, baking powder, and salt.
4. Add dry ingredients to wet mixture. Mix thoroughly until batter is smooth. Blend in poppy seeds.
5. Grease three 9-inch round cake pans. (One time I made 2 cakes, 2 mini loaves, and a 4½-by-8½-inch tea loaf. I like to bake several different shapes.) Bake 1 hour until a light golden tan. Cool ½ hour.
6. Serve each slice plain, or with a dollop of whipped cream and a sprinkle of lemon zest. For extra "insects" add a few more poppy seeds on top.

Yield: 3 round cake layers (or several different shapes).

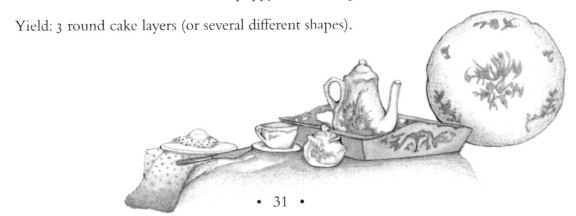

EASTER

*T*he Easter holiday begins forty days prior to Easter Sunday (the date varies between March and April) with Ash Wednesday, the beginning of a period called Lent. During the forty days of Lent, many people give up favorite foods in commemoration of the forty days Jesus of Nazareth spent praying in the wilderness prior to his death. When Jesus and his twelve disciples went out to spread his teachings, Jesus rode into Jerusalem on a donkey. (Jesus and his followers were Jews, and they were in the city to celebrate the Passover holiday. Pasch, another name for Easter, is derived from Pesach, Hebrew for Passover.) Crowds gathered, waving palm branches to welcome him. Palm Sunday, which commemorates this day, is a week before Easter. Good Friday, two days prior to Easter, marks the day Jesus died. One of his disciples, Judas, betrayed him to the Roman rulers after the Last Supper, which was a Passover meal. Christians believe Easter Sunday is the day Jesus rose from the dead and ascended to heaven. They go to church to honor him as their savior and Messiah and celebrate his eternal life.

Easter is also a celebration of spring. Long before Easter, there was an ancient Anglo-Saxon festival for the goddess of spring, Eostre, who is often seen with a hare by her side. The rabbit symbolizes fertility. Customs from that festival have become a part of Easter. In many cultures the egg is a symbol of new life and rebirth. The Easter Bunny delivers baskets full of chocolate eggs wrapped in foil, decorated eggs, and jelly beans; sometimes he hides eggs that have to be found during an Easter egg hunt. Some people have egg-rolling contests or stroll in parades wearing fancy Easter bonnets. But most important, families join together in a Sunday meal of remembrance and joy.

EASTER

Decorating Easter Eggs
E. Bunny's Chopped Egg Salad
Hot Cross Breakfast Buns
Sunday Roast Lamb

Decorating Easter Eggs

The ancient Chinese, Persians, and northern Europeans during the Middle Ages all gave eggs as gifts during spring festivals. In Poland and the Ukraine, detailed designs are handpainted on eggs with beeswax, and then the eggs are dipped in dye. After the dye is dry, the wax is melted and the design, in the natural color of the egg, remains. Their Easter eggs are known throughout the world. In 1885, Fabergé, the Russian jeweler and goldsmith, became famous for making jeweled Easter eggs for the czar. The custom of hanging decorated eggs on trees came to America with the German settlers. While boiling eggs for egg salad, boil a few extras to decorate!

This is how to make them:

1. In a large saucepan put enough water to cover white eggs. Boil for 15 minutes. Remove from heat and put eggs in cold water to cool. Draw designs on the eggs with crayons, paint them with acrylic paints, or wrap rubber bands around them.
2. With a soupspoon, dip eggs in food coloring or natural-colored vegetable dyes, such as beet juice. The dye won't adhere to the egg where the crayon, paint, or rubber band has been applied.
3. To get mixed colors and patterns, remove rubber bands, redecorate, and dip again into another color. Allow eggs to dry in an egg carton.

E. Bunny's Chopped Egg Salad

In an E-mail message to the Easter Bunny, Mrs. Claus happened to mention Santa's cholesterol count, and his "healthy" appetite. It just so happened that the Easter Bunny had similar problems years before (his friends used to call him "Easter Tummy"). So in response he sent Mrs. Claus a recipe for egg salad that called for more egg whites than yolks. "With all the hopping around I do, I get a good aerobic workout. It's easier for me to lose my paunch," he added. "Santa sits in his sleigh a lot." "Well, he does do some rappelling down the chimney," Mrs. Claus said, "but I agree, less is more."

1 dozen extra large eggs
4 tablespoons low-fat mayonnaise
1 teaspoon ground pepper
Pinch of paprika (optional)
Sprigs of curly parsley and sweet red pepper strips to garnish

1. In a large pot on stove, place eggs in enough water to cover them completely. Boil for 15 minutes or until cracks appear on shells. Discard water.
2. Place eggs in a bowl of cold water for 5 minutes. Knock top of egg on a hard surface to crack shell. Carefully remove and discard shells. Wash eggs under faucet. Put in dry bowl. Remove and discard 5 yolks (the yellow centers). Mash eggs with a fork. Add mayonnaise. Mix.
3. Make a mound of egg salad on a platter. Sprinkle with pepper and paprika. Dot with parsley and place red pepper strips around the outside of the mound.

Yield: Serves 8 little "bunnies" or 6 regular-size ones.

Hot Cross Breakfast Buns

This sweet bun has become a traditional Easter food because it has a cross of icing on top.

Buns
1 teaspoon granulated sugar (for yeast)
¼ cup warm water (105°–115°F)
1 package active dry yeast
1 cup milk
¼ cup butter
½ cup granulated sugar
½ teaspoon salt
½ teaspoon nutmeg
1 teaspoon cinnamon

1 teaspoon orange zest
2 large eggs (reserve 1 yolk)
4 cups unbleached flour, sifted
¾ cup dark raisins or currants
1 teaspoon cold water

Icing
1 tablespoon milk
1 cup confectioners' sugar
½ teaspoon vanilla extract

1. *Buns:* In a small bowl, dissolve 1 teaspoon sugar in warm water. Add yeast. Set aside for 10 minutes at room temperature until liquid foams.
2. In a small pot on stove, scald milk (heat until foamy), adding butter, sugar, salt, nutmeg, cinnamon, and grated orange zest. Cool to lukewarm. Beat eggs. Add to pot and stir.
3. In a large mixing bowl, combine by hand yeast with milk mixture. Gradually add flour (saving about ½ cup). Stir in raisins. Knead dough until elastic. Cover with dish towel and put in a warm spot. Let dough rise until double in size (for about 2 hours). Punch down.
4. Dip fingers in flour. Rip dough and roll by hand into plum-size balls. Set buns on parchment-lined cookie sheet. When half risen (after about ½ hour), make a cross ⅜ inch deep on top of bun with a sharp knife. Allow to rise again to twice the original size. With a pastry brush, brush on glaze of reserved egg yolk mixed with 1 teaspoon cold water.
5. Preheat oven to 375° and bake 20–30 minutes until golden brown.
6. *Icing:* Whisk together milk, confectioners' sugar, and vanilla. Drip icing inside cross while still warm.

Yield: Around 2 dozen.

Hot cross buns, hot cross buns,
One a penny, two a penny,
Hot cross buns.
Smoking hot, piping hot,
Just come out of the baker's shop;
One a penny poke, two a penny tongs,
Three a penny fire-shovel,
Hot cross buns!

—Nursery rhyme shouted by English street vendors on Good Friday

Sunday Roast Lamb

The tradition of lamb at Easter has its roots in the story of the Exodus. God sent the Angel of Death to kill the firstborn sons of Egypt when Pharaoh refused to let the Hebrew slaves leave. Moses told the Hebrews to mark their doorways with the blood of a newborn lamb so that the Angel of Death would pass over their homes. For centuries after, there was a yearly sacrifice of paschal lambs. To the early Christians, this became associated with the sacrifice of Jesus. Jesus, often depicted as the Good Shepherd, carrying a staff and a baby lamb, is also referred to as the Lamb of God.

7-pound leg (or shoulder) of lamb
2 tablespoons spicy brown mustard
1 tablespoon lemon juice
1 tablespoon balsamic vinegar
2 tablespoons water
2 teaspoons rosemary (or 3 sprigs)
1 bulb garlic, cloves peeled

20 new potatoes (red or white)
1 stalk celery, finely diced
2 dozen baby Belgian carrots
2 McIntosh apples, peeled, cored, and quartered
1 jar or 8 fresh artichoke hearts
1 small jar mint jelly

1. Preheat oven to 400°.
2. Put lamb in large roasting pan. Brush lamb with mixture of mustard, lemon juice, vinegar, and water. Season meat by rubbing it with rosemary and garlic. Roast 30–45 minutes in a covered pan.
3. Rotate lamb, and add to roasting pan potatoes, celery, carrots, apples, and artichokes. Continue to roast in uncovered pan an additional ½ hour.
4. Display lamb on a platter outlined with vegetables. Serve sliced with mint jelly on the side for dipping.

Yield: Serves 8.

PASSOVER

Passover begins during March or April (on the 15th of Nisan, according to the Jewish calendar) and lasts eight days. It is called the Festival of Freedom, commemorating the Exodus of the Israelites from slavery in Egypt. Pharaoh, ruler of Egypt, refused to let the Jewish people go, and God brought ten plagues upon the Egyptians. With the last plague—the killing of the firstborn—Pharaoh finally allowed the Jews their freedom. The Hebrew people left in such haste, their bread did not have time to rise. Unleavened bread called "matzoh" is eaten during Passover in remembrance. The holiday begins the night before, when the family searches the house for any remaining "chametz," or foods that can't be eaten during Passover. While holding a candle, they use a wooden spoon and a feather to sweep up any crumbs.

The holiday is celebrated with a ritual family meal called a "seder," in which customs are done in a specific order ("seder" literally means "order"). The readings, prayers, and practices of a seder are in a book called a "Haggadah," which recounts the meaning of the Exodus through story and song. Every person at the table participates in the ceremony. Each food on the seder plate has a special significance.

PASSOVER

The Seder Plate
Apple-and-Walnut Ḥaroset
Date-and-Almond Ḥaroset
Vegetarian Matzoh Ball Soup
Classic Brisket
Fanny's Flourless Chocolate Cake

The Seder Plate

1. Egg (*beitzah*): The roasted egg recalls the time when sacrificial offerings were made in the Temple in Jerusalem. The egg is also a symbol of fertility and new life.

2. Shank bone (*zeroa*): A burnt portion of a lamb leg bone represents the paschal offering, also in memory of the ancient Temple sacrifice.

3. Bitter herbs (*maror*): Usually horseradish, sometimes romaine lettuce. Signifies the bitterness of slavery in Egypt.

4. *Ḥaroset*: Sweet paste of chopped apples, nuts, and cinnamon mixed with a sweet red wine. The fruit-and-nut mixture symbolizes the mortar and bricks the Israelites used to build pyramids when they were in bondage to the pharaohs in Egypt. The red wine is a reminder that God parted the Red Sea during the Exodus.

5. Parsley (*karpas*): A sprig of parsley stands for spring, life, and hope. Parsley dipped in salt water suggests the salty tears of the slaves.

6. Grated horseradish (*ḥazeret*): Additional bitter herb eaten with the *ḥaroset* in *matzoh* sandwich (*koreḥ*). Shows life has two sides—bitter and sweet.

7. *Matzoh*: Unleavened bread is a reminder that the Hebrews left Egypt in such haste, the bread didn't have time to rise. Three *matzot* on a separate plate, covered with a special cloth and placed in the center of the table, represent the three tribes of Israel. The *afikomen* (a Greek word meaning "dessert") is the middle *matzoh,* which is hidden during the seder. Children search for it later on in the meal, and the one who finds it gets a little treat.

The Seder Plate

Apple-and-Walnut Ḥaroset

Ashkenazi Jews, or Jews from eastern Europe, eat this kind of ḥaroset.

4 cups shelled walnuts

5 cups sweet apples, peeled and chopped

Peel of 1 lemon, finely grated

1½ teaspoons cinnamon

¾ cup Concord grape wine
    or grape juice

1 tablespoon maple syrup or
    granulated sugar (to taste)

1. In a food processor, chop nuts (or pound by hand with a mortar and pestle). Mix all ingredients into a paste. (I like a chunkier consistency and do not chop the walnuts very fine.) Put in a bowl and chill before serving.
2. During the seder, the ḥaroset is spread on small pieces of broken matzoh.

Yield: Serves 50, depending on whether your guests like to "heap" or *schmeer*. Enough for two seders.

Date-and-Almond Ḥaroset

Sephardic Jews, whose ancestors came from Spain, Portugal, and Middle Eastern countries, where dates and figs are bountiful, eat different kinds of ḥaroset. My family was at a seder in Morocco, where the leader mashed a large ball of dates in a bowl with a fork, while adding wine. This ḥaroset was served wrapped in romaine lettuce (for the bitter herbs), and also on small pieces of matzoh.

½ cup blanched almonds

1½ cups pitted dates, chopped

½ cup figs, chopped

½ teaspoon orange zest

½ teaspoon cinnamon

¼ teaspoon coriander

¼ teaspoon ground cloves

¼ teaspoon ginger

Pinch of cayenne pepper

Pinch of allspice

1 teaspoon lemon juice

⅓ cup sweet red wine

In a food processor, chop nuts first. Then blend dates, figs, orange zest, and spices together to form a sticky mass. Roll into 2-inch balls. Put in bowl. Gradually add lemon juice and wine to mixture, making a thick paste. Chill if not used immediately.

Yield: Serves about 40 (20 guests for each night's seder!).

Vegetarian Matzoh Ball Soup

The usual schmaltz—chicken fat—is absent from the matzoh balls in this low-calorie, lighter version of the classic chicken soup recipe. Many Mediterranean Jews eat leeks during the Passover season.

Soup

12 cups water
2 carrots, peeled and cut into ⅜-inch slices
1 celery heart (center stalk with all leaves), sliced
1 medium parsnip, cut into ½-inch slices
1 parsley root with greens, or ⅓ cup fresh parsley, chopped
1 white base of large leek, quartered lengthwise
1 large onion, peeled and quartered
1 cup cabbage, chopped
½ zucchini, sliced thin
Salt and pepper to taste
4 whole cloves of garlic, peeled
4 green cardamom seeds
Sprigs of parsley or dill to garnish

Matzoh balls

2 large eggs, beaten
Salt and pepper to taste
1 cup matzoh meal
¾–1 cup seltzer

1. *Soup*: Add all ingredients to a very large soup pot. Simmer over low flame for 1½–2 hours. When soup stock is done, to thicken consommé before serving, take 2 cups of the vegetables out of the soup, along with some liquid, and purée in blender for about 1 minute, then add back to soup pot. While cooking the soup, make the matzoh balls.
2. *Matzoh balls*: In a small bowl, beat eggs, salt, and pepper. Add matzoh meal and mix by hand. Stir in seltzer, and continue to mix while seltzer is foaming with matzoh meal. Cover. Refrigerate 1 hour.
3. Form Ping-Pong-size matzoh balls, dipping fingers into bowl of water before rolling each matzoh ball to make balls smooth.
4. Drop balls one by one into boiling water or into soup (either method is fine). Cover pot. Simmer 15 minutes (last 15 minutes of soup cooking time if in soup).
5. Sprinkle each bowl of soup with freshly chopped parsley or dill.

Yield: Serves 8.

Classic Brisket

Passover would not be Passover without a brisket. Everybody has their own version. This is mine.

1 first-cut kosher beef brisket (about 7 pounds)
½ teaspoon paprika
8–10 ounces ketchup
2 tablespoons grape jelly
4–6 plum tomatoes
1 medium onion, peeled and chopped

8–10 garlic cloves, peeled
2 celery stalks, cut into 1-inch slices
3 carrots, peeled and cut into 1-inch slices
2 dozen new potatoes (red or white)
1 tablespoon fresh parsley, chopped

1. In a very large pot on stove top, put brisket, sprinkled with paprika, in a sauce of ketchup and jelly. Put tomatoes, onion, and garlic on and around meat. Cook partially covered over low heat 1½ hours. Then add other vegetables. Continue to simmer additional ½ hour.

2. Remove brisket from pot. Slice against the grain into thin strips and return to pot. Refrigerate. Skim fat. (I make it the day before.)

3. Preheat oven to 400°. Place brisket in covered baking dish. Heat for ½ hour until meat is brown and tender in the tomato sauce. Garnish with parsley and serve.

Yield: Serves about 8 (brisket shrinks when cooked).

Fanny's Flourless Chocolate Cake

This cake is a nice change from the typical macaroons and sponge cake usually served at Passover. Note: Passover cake meal is different from matzoh meal.

½ cup unsalted margarine
6 ounces semisweet chocolate
½ cup light brown sugar
4 extra large eggs, separated
1 teaspoon vanilla extract

¼ teaspoon cinnamon
⅓ cup Passover cake meal
Pinch of salt (optional)
⅓ cup walnuts or hazelnuts, crushed
1 tablespoon cocoa powder

1. Preheat oven to 375°.
2. In a double boiler, melt margarine and chocolate. (See page 19 for other ways to melt butter and chocolate.) Stir in sugar to dissolve. Set aside and allow to cool to room temperature.
3. Beat egg yolks in mixing bowl, adding vanilla, cinnamon, and cake meal. With electric mixer at high speed, add chocolate mixture.
4. In a separate bowl with clean beaters, beat egg whites and salt until stiff peaks form. Gently fold egg whites into batter with a spatula, slowly adding crushed nuts.
5. Grease 9-inch round springform cake pan with margarine, and dust with cocoa powder. Pour in batter and bake 30–40 minutes.

Yield: 1 9-inch round cake (pareve and kosher for Passover).

MOTHER'S DAY

Mother's Day was first suggested in 1872 by a writer named Julia Ward Howe. Then, in 1907, another woman, Anna Jarvis, began an energetic letter-writing campaign to politicians and clergy. She lobbied for a special day to be set aside to celebrate motherhood. Seven years later, on May 9, 1914, Congress declared Mother's Day an official holiday. It is traditionally celebrated on the second Sunday in May. We honor our mothers by giving them cards, flowers, gifts, and special treats like breakfast in bed.

MOTHER'S DAY

Fluffy Cinnamon French Toast
Mama's Mocha Truffles
Chocolate-Dipped Strawberries

Fluffy Cinnamon French Toast

Challah, *an egg-enriched bread used for the Jewish Sabbath, can be found in many bakeries. It is absorbent and makes a fluffy French toast. Substitute raisin bread if challah isn't available.*

2 large eggs, beaten
¼ cup low-fat milk
½ teaspoon vanilla extract
1 large raisin challah loaf

1 tablespoon cinnamon
Margarine or butter for frying
Confectioners' sugar (optional)
Maple syrup or raspberry jam

1. In a large bowl, beat eggs with milk, vanilla, and cinnamon.
2. Cut challah in ¾-inch wedges. Soak in egg mixture in bowl until soggy.
3. In a large frying pan, melt butter over medium flame and fry bread on each side 4–5 minutes or until lightly browned.
4. Put toast on a plate. Dust lightly with confectioners' sugar. Serve with maple syrup or raspberry jam. (Personally, I love it with maple syrup that my husband makes from tapping the trees in our own backyard, and a dab of cottage cheese on the side!)

Yield: Serves about 4–6.

Mama's Mocha Truffles

1 pound semisweet chocolate
1 teaspoon ground instant coffee
¾ cup butter or margarine
¾ cup fresh cream

3 tablespoons confectioners' sugar
Cocoa powder for dusting candy
Pinch of cinnamon in cocoa (optional)

1. Melt chocolate in double boiler. Add coffee when melted. Stir.
2. Melt butter in same pot as chocolate and continue to stir. Remove from stove. Gradually add cream, then sugar. Mix thoroughly.
3. In a covered bowl, cool mixture in refrigerator to harden slightly.
4. When it becomes doughlike, roll it with your hands into grape-size balls. Coat each one with a fine dusting of cocoa powder. Serve at room temperature.

Yield: Depends on size of balls you make.

Chocolate-Dipped Strawberries

Chocolate-dipped fruit is a special treat for someone you love. Melt white, milk, bittersweet, or semisweet baking chocolate and dip dried apricots, pears, mangoes, crystallized ginger, pineapple, ripe banana slices, or fresh grapes, and of course, non-fruit items like marshmallows, Oreo cookies, or small pretzels. (For Valentine's Day or Independence Day, dip the fresh red strawberries into white chocolate.)

1 pound semisweet chocolate
1 pat unsalted butter
1 pint fresh strawberries (or your choice of fruit)

1. On top of stove in double boiler, melt chocolate over hot water. (See page 19 for other ways to melt chocolate.) Stir until smooth.
2. Add a small pat of butter if chocolate is too thick, and stir.
3. Wash and dry strawberries, leaving green top on berries.
4. Using a fork, gently spear fruit and lower halfway into melted chocolate. Lift out, quickly rotating berry so the bottom half is thoroughly covered. Drain excess chocolate back into pot. Place on rack or plate covered with wax paper. Chill in refrigerator to harden.
5. Tuck each strawberry into a tiny paper bonbon cup, if available. Serve.

MEMORIAL DAY

Memorial Day honors everyone who has ever died serving our country in wartime. The holiday was established after the American Civil War. On May 5, 1866, Henry C. Welles, a druggist from Waterloo, New York, honored those who had died in war by decorating their graves with flowers and flags. Another man, General John A. Logan, organized a group of veterans from the North called the "Grand Army of the Republic." On May 30, 1868, Welles and Logan joined forces to observe what they called "Decoration Day." In 1882, Decoration Day became Memorial Day, but it wasn't until 1971 that it was declared a national legal holiday, taking place on the last Monday of May. The date varies each year according to the calendar.

Today we mark the day in much the same way it was marked over a hundred years ago: with big parades in which everyone waves small American flags; band concerts; and public fireworks displays. Families often celebrate the long weekend with barbecues in backyards or picnics in parks, relishing the fact that summer's around the corner.

MEMORIAL DAY

Waldorf Salad
Cucumber, Yogurt, and Mint Salad
Orange Couscous
Wild Rice Pilaf
Sweet and Sour Meatballs
Veteran's Vegetable Kebabs

Waldorf Salad

This healthy salad is perfect for any picnic or barbecue.

1 medium red cabbage

4 carrots, peeled

3 McIntosh apples, cut into bite-size pieces

¾ cup dark raisins or currants

1 tablespoon honey or granulated sugar

½ cup apple cider vinegar

½ cup mayonnaise

Pinch of allspice

1. Shred cabbage and carrots. Put in large mixing bowl. Add apples and raisins or currants.
2. In a separate bowl dissolve honey or sugar in vinegar. Add mayonnaise and allspice. Stir dressing. Pour over salad. Mix thoroughly.
3. Refrigerate until chilled. Serve cold as a side dish.

Yield: Serves about 8–10.

Cucumber, Yogurt, and Mint Salad

2 cucumbers, peeled

1 cup plain yogurt

½ cup dark raisins

2 tablespoons fresh mint, chopped

1. Dice cucumbers. Put in bowl and coat with yogurt.
2. Add raisins and mint. Stir with a large spoon. Chill before serving.

Yield: Serves 6.

Orange Couscous

Couscous is a tiny pale yellow grainlike pasta made from wheat. It is wonderful with any kind of kebab and can be found in a Middle Eastern or health food store, and in many supermarkets. Italian pignolia nuts are sold in most supermarkets or specialty groceries. They are often used on top of cookies, but they make a nice addition here.

2½ cups water

1 cup couscous

½ teaspoon curry (optional)

1 tablespoon olive oil

1 cup canned mandarin oranges

¼ cup light raisins

2 tablespoons pignolia nuts (optional)

Finely chopped fresh parsley to garnish

1. In medium pot, bring water to boil. Reduce heat. Add couscous and curry. Allow to simmer for 5–10 minutes, covered.
2. Add olive oil, mandarin oranges, raisins, and nuts. Fluff with fork.
3. Put in pretty bowl. Garnish with parsley. Serve at room temperature.

Yield: Serves 6–8.

Wild Rice Pilaf

This rice makes a nice bed on which to display your vegetable kebabs.

½ cup wild rice

Salt to taste (optional)

5 cups water

1½ cups white or brown rice

¼ cup pilaf noodles

⅓ cup slivered almonds

1. In a covered pot, add wild rice and salt to boiling water. Continue to boil over a medium flame for 15 minutes.
2. Add white or brown rice and pilaf noodles. Boil for another 10 minutes.
3. Turn off burner. Add almonds. Fluff mixture and leave covered on stove top 10 minutes.
4. The rice and pilaf should be plump now. Fluff again. Serve hot or at room temperature.

Yield: Serves 6–8.

Sweet and Sour Meatballs

Put a cup of toothpicks in the center of a platter of meatballs and watch people pop the meatballs one by one into their mouths. If you want them spicy and hot like firecrackers, add about 1 teaspoon of chili powder to meat!

2 slices sandwich bread (any kind)	1 large egg, beaten
6 tablespoons boiling water	½ cup ketchup
1 package (1.4 ounces) onion soup mix	¼ cup grape jelly
3½ pounds hamburger meat	2 cups water (for sauce)
½ teaspoon garlic powder	3 garlic cloves, peeled and minced

1. In a large mixing bowl, soften bread with water; add soup mix. Mix in meat, garlic powder, and egg. Mash thoroughly with a fork.
2. Roll into small walnut-size meatballs, dipping fingers every so often into a bowl of cold water to make meatballs round and smooth.
3. In a large covered pot on stove top, heat ketchup, jelly, water, and garlic for 5 minutes, stirring sauce. Add meatballs one by one and simmer 45 minutes over medium flame, carefully turning them with a wooden spoon every 15 minutes so they won't stick to the bottom of the pot. Serve hot.

Yield: 8 dozen.

Veteran's Vegetable Kebabs

For vegetarians, any barbecue can be a toughie. Here's a dish that will please vegetarian and meat eaters alike. Chicken, beef, or lamb can always be added to your kebab. Use stainless steel skewers or disposable wooden ones.

1 pound tofu (firm kind)

2 large red peppers

2 large green peppers

2 large yellow peppers

1 large onion, peeled and quartered

1 large zucchini, cut into ½-inch slices

1 yellow squash, cut into ½-inch slices

2 dozen mushroom caps

Pineapple chunks

1 pint cherry tomatoes

1. Cut tofu and peppers into bite-size pieces. (Cut peppers into about 2-inch-wide strips and then cut again in half.) Put in large mixing bowl. Add onion, zucchini, and squash. Marinate for about 1 hour in marinade.

2. *Marinade*: 1 small can orange juice concentrate, ½ cup soy sauce, 2 tablespoons honey, 1 teaspoon ground ginger, ½ teaspoon garlic powder, and ¼ cup olive oil (optional).

3. Take stems off mushrooms and use only caps. Cut pineapple into bite-size chunks. For each skewer alternate pieces, piercing center of each piece of tofu, vegetable, or pineapple, ending with a cherry tomato. Repeat the order if there is room on the skewer. (See diagram.)

4. Grill each side on medium flame for about 5 minutes until vegetables are tender. If meat is added, grill until meat is cooked.

Yield: Serves 12–14.

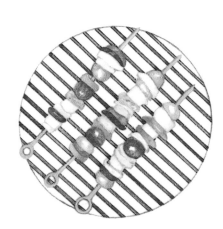

FATHER'S DAY

The idea for Father's Day originated with Mrs. John Bruce Dodd of Spokane, Washington. On the third Sunday of June in 1910, she suggested that people wear a red rose to church to honor a father who was alive, and a white rose if he was not. The custom of honoring our fathers is celebrated the same way today by many families throughout America. Children, grandchildren, and wives write greeting cards, give presents, and have big dinners or barbecues together to show appreciation for their dad.

On this special day my father always loved to make pancakes. My husband has continued the tradition with waffles. Of course, you can make them for your father with some help.

June is warm and sunny. Dig your toes into the earth. Help your father plant flowers and vegetables in the garden or window box. Share chocolate chip cookies and iced lemonade afterward.

FATHER'S DAY

Belgian Waffles and Blueberry Pancakes
Chocolate Chip Cookies
Papa's Lemonade

Belgian Waffles and Blueberry Pancakes

This batter can be used to make either waffles or pancakes. The combined dry ingredients can be stored in a glass jar or large plastic bag for later use. During the 1964 World's Fair, I tasted Belgian waffles, dripping with strawberries, for the first time. You can decorate these with a dollop of whipped cream and fresh or thawed frozen strawberries. Or you can make pancakes with fresh blueberries mixed in the batter. My father made blueberry pancakes on Sunday mornings, and I always think of him when I eat them.

1 cup unbleached flour, sifted

¼ teaspoon salt

1 teaspoon baking powder

¼ cup cornmeal (optional)

1 large egg, beaten

1 cup milk or buttermilk

1 tablespoon sour cream or yogurt

Butter for frying

Strawberries and whipped cream

Blueberries and maple syrup

1. Sift dry ingredients into a large bowl.
2. Mix in wet ingredients. Stir until the batter is smooth. If cornmeal is used as well, add an additional ¼ cup of milk.
3. *For waffles:* Grease waffle iron and ladle batter into each section. Remove waffles when light golden brown, or when the light goes off! (We use an old black wrought-iron waffle pan that we have from when my husband was a Boy Scout.) Serve with strawberries and whipped cream.
4. *For pancakes:* Add ½ cup of blueberries to batter. Ladle circles onto greased pan. Cook pancakes over medium heat until little bubbles form on top. Flip pancakes and cook on other side until light golden brown. Serve with maple syrup.

Yield: 3 9-inch waffles or 10 5-inch pancakes.

Chocolate Chip Cookies

On top of each chewy cookie place a giant-size chocolate chip or chocolate chunk—to give Dad an extra treat!

2 cups unbleached flour, sifted
1 teaspoon baking soda
¼ teaspoon salt
½ cup butter or margarine, softened
1 teaspoon vanilla extract

½ cup granulated sugar
½ cup dark brown sugar
2 large eggs, beaten
1 cup chocolate chips
1 cup chopped walnuts (optional)

1. Preheat oven to 375°.
2. Sift flour, baking soda, and salt into bowl. Set aside.
3. In another bowl use electric mixer to cream butter (or margarine) with vanilla. Add both sugars and eggs. Gradually add flour mixture. Stir thoroughly until smooth. Mix in chips and, if desired, walnuts.
4. On a parchment-lined or greased cookie sheet, drop teaspoonfuls of dough spaced about 2 inches apart.
5. In the center of each cookie, place 1 large chocolate morsel or walnut. Bake 10 minutes. Remove with a spatula. Put on rack or plate to cool.

Yield: 4 dozen chunky 2-inch cookies.

Papa's Lemonade

For each glass of water add: 1–2 tablespoons freshly squeezed lemon juice, 2 tablespoons granulated sugar (or honey) dissolved in a small amount of boiling water, pinch of salt. Decorate each glass of lemonade with thin lemon slice. Serve over ice.

INDEPENDENCE DAY

This holiday, also called "Fourth of July," commemorates the adoption of the Declaration of Independence by the Continental Congress in Philadelphia on July 4, 1776. Thomas Jefferson wrote this document on behalf of the Continental Congress to proclaim the colonies' independence from King George III of England. A copy of the Declaration was sent to General George Washington, and he read it to his ragtag colonial soldiers, who had fought bravely against British troops during the Revolutionary War. Bells rang and cannons roared as news spread throughout the land. Bands played and bonfires soared, celebrating the words that "all men are created equal" and everyone has the right to "life, liberty and the pursuit of happiness." The United States was built on these principles. The Fourth of July was declared a legal holiday in 1941, during World War II.

The day is traditionally celebrated with patriotic speeches, parades with marching bands, firecrackers, and red-white-and-blue flags waving. There are family picnics with watermelon-eating or egg-tossing contests, old-fashioned cotton candy, and burlap potato-sack races. Some towns hold pageants in which people reenact the days of the Revolutionary War in period costumes. The highlight of the holiday comes at night, when people gather to sing "The Star-Spangled Banner" and watch colorful and noisy fireworks displays.

INDEPENDENCE DAY

Firecracker Potato Salad
Stars and Stripes Fusilli
Patriotic Cheesecake
All-American Fruit Salad

Firecracker Potato Salad

Make this side dish to hamburgers, hot dogs, or chicken for a Fourth of July picnic or barbecue. If you want it firecracker hot, add 1 small chopped jalapeño pepper!

6 large Idaho potatoes

½ cup mayonnaise

3 tablespoons apple cider vinegar

1 large red pepper, finely chopped

⅓ cup Italian parsley or cilantro, finely chopped

1 teaspoon paprika

1. In a large pot, boil potatoes in skins about 45 minutes until tender. (Spear center gently with a skewer or fork to check.) Cool 5 minutes in cold water. Peel and rinse potatoes. Cut into medium chunks or thin slices. Put in large mixing bowl.

2. In a measuring cup, stir mayonnaise and apple cider vinegar with a fork. Pour over potatoes, adding red pepper and parsley. Mix together. (I use Italian parsley instead of the curly sprigs for more zip, and cilantro if I want it even zippier!) Put on plate or in a bowl and sprinkle paprika on top.

3. Serve at room temperature, or refrigerate and serve chilled.

Yield: Serves 12–14 (depending on whether your guests are big eaters!).

Stars and Stripes Fusilli

Like the stars and stripes of the American flag, everything in this platter is red or white.

2 red peppers

4 plum tomatoes, diced

1 cup white kidney or cannellini beans, canned or dried

¼ teaspoon garlic powder

Vegetable oil for sautéing

Pinch of red cayenne pepper

10 cauliflower florets

1 pound fusilli pasta

1. Wash and slice peppers into ⅜-inch strips, discarding seeds. Roast peppers in 400° oven until tender. Set aside.
2. In a medium frying pan, sauté tomatoes and beans in garlic and oil. (Note: If beans are dried, presoak in 2 cups of water until beans swell. Boil about 1 hour or until beans are tender.)
3. Steam cauliflower until tender. Mix with tomato mixture in pan.
4. Boil fusilli until soft but firm. Put on platter.
5. Spoon tomatoes, beans, and cauliflower onto fusilli. Toss gently, adding cayenne pepper. Serve warm or at room temperature.

Yield: Serves 6–8.

Patriotic Cheesecake

This cheesecake is the three colors of the American flag:
red: strawberries, raspberries, or cherries
white: cheesecake
blue: blueberries

Crust
1¾ cups graham cracker crumbs

¼ cup confectioners' sugar, sifted

2 teaspoons cinnamon

1 teaspoon orange zest (optional)

6–7 tablespoons butter, melted

Filling
8 ounces cream cheese, softened

1 cup reduced-fat sour cream

2 teaspoons vanilla extract

2 large eggs, beaten

2 tablespoons confectioners' sugar

1. *Crust:* Break graham crackers into small pieces. Grind them in a blender until they are crushed into crumbs. (Or buy box of crumbs already ground.) Add sugar, cinnamon, and orange zest. Mix in bowl.
2. Pour in melted butter and mix thoroughly. Press crumbs into a 9-inch pie pan or spring-form cake pan. Set crust aside. (Crumb crust hardens after it is baked.)
3. Preheat oven to 350°.
4. *Filling:* With an electric mixer mix all ingredients in a large bowl.
5. Pour filling into crust. Bake for 1 hour. Turn off oven. Leave cake in oven for additional hour to cool, with oven door open a crack.
6. Cover with plastic wrap and chill in refrigerator overnight.
7. Before serving, decorate top with fresh blueberries and sliced strawberries. Serve with whipped cream.

Yield: 12 red-white-and-blue slices.

All-American Fruit Salad

Use any fruit that is red, white, or blue and combine in a watermelon "boat." Serve this festive dessert chilled. For a refreshing addition on a hot day, add a scoop of lemon, raspberry, or boysenberry sherbert or sorbet.

Red	White	Blue
1 watermelon	3 ripe bananas	1 pint blueberries
1 pint strawberries	1 honeydew melon	Dark purple grapes
1 pint raspberries	1 large pineapple	3 dark purple plums
½ cup pitted cherries	2 cups grapefruit	Blackberries or
3 sweet apples	Shredded coconut	boysenberries

1. Cut watermelon in half. Scoop out inside with a melon baller, or use a knife to make bite-size chunks. Remove seeds. Set melon aside.
2. Wash all berries and cherries. Slice strawberries and take green stems off top. Core and cut apples into small pieces. Peel and slice bananas. Set all fruit aside in a bowl.
3. Cut honeydew melon in half. Discard seeds. Scoop out melon balls or cut into small bite-size chunks. Set aside.
4. Cut rind off pineapple, and cut into bite-size chunks.
5. Buy grapefruit sections, or peel fresh grapefruit, and section, discarding any skin and seeds.
6. Wash medium bunch of grapes. Pluck each grape off the stem.
7. Wash and cut plums into small pieces (leave skin on). Discard pits.
8. Combine and mix all fruit inside the watermelon "boat." Sprinkle with shredded coconut flakes.

Yield: Serves 20 or more.

LABOR DAY

*L*abor Day was first suggested in the late nineteenth century by Peter J. McGuire, general secretary of the United Brotherhood of Carpenters and Joiners of America, a labor union. He wanted the first Monday of September to be a day of rest for the labor force in our country. On September 5, 1882, the Knights of Labor held a large parade in New York City to honor workers. After the parade there was a large picnic and later that evening a fireworks display—customs that remain today. At a labor meeting held in Chicago on October 9, 1884, workers voted for a national holiday. One by one, many states (Oregon being the first, in 1887) instituted laws to make this Monday a holiday; it wasn't until 1894 that the United States Congress designated it a legal holiday.

Labor Day weekend marks the end of summer and vacation. It is celebrated with parades, country fairs, baseball or soccer games, fireworks, picnics, family outings to parks or beaches, or just resting in the backyard. People still like to eat the kinds of foods their relatives enjoyed more than a hundred years ago—apple pie, peach cobbler, chicken, fresh-baked bread, and toasted marshmallows, to name a few.

LABOR DAY

Laid-Back Banana Bread
Easy Chicken Salad
Virtual Burgers
Old-Fashioned Peach Cobbler
September S'mores

Laid-Back Banana Bread

Almost everyone has an overripe banana or two hanging around the kitchen. You stare at it over your breakfast cereal. You don't want to eat it, but you don't want to waste it either. So here's a good use for that banana. It's quick and easy to make for a holiday of rest. If you really want *to take it easy, you can bake the bread ahead of time, freeze it, thaw, and reheat.*

2 cups unbleached flour, sifted
2 teaspoons baking powder
½ teaspoon baking soda
5 tablespoons butter, softened
½–¾ cup granulated sugar
1 teaspoon maple syrup (optional)
3 tablespoons sour cream or yogurt

1 teaspoon lemon zest
1 large egg, beaten
2 average-size ripe bananas
1 teaspoon vanilla extract
½ cup chopped walnuts
4 walnut halves

1. Preheat oven to 350°.
2. In a large bowl, sift flour, baking powder, and baking soda. Set aside.
3. In another bowl, cream softened butter and sugar with electric mixer. Gradually add maple syrup, sour cream, lemon zest, egg, bananas, and vanilla until mixture is smooth. Mix in chopped walnuts.
4. Pour batter into a 4½-by-8½-inch greased bread pan. (Disposable aluminum pans can be found in the baking section of the supermarket.)
5. Decorate top of bread with four walnut halves. Bake 1 hour or until a skewer put in the center of the loaf comes up dry. Then you know it's done!

Yield: 1 large loaf (plus enough batter left for 2 small 2½-by-5-inch loaves to give as a little gift to someone who works hard!).

Easy Chicken Salad

Whenever I have leftover boiled chicken from making chicken soup, I make this recipe, but you don't have to make soup first. Any cooked, skinned, and boned chicken or cutlets will do.

4 cups cooked chicken	Optional ingredients
3 tablespoons mayonnaise	1 apple, peeled and diced
1 stalk celery, finely diced	¼ cup light raisins
2 teaspoons fresh tarragon, chopped	¼ cup chopped walnuts

1. Cut cooked, boned chicken into bite-size pieces. (If you prefer the "mashed style," use a fork. I like small sliced chunks.)
2. In a mixing bowl, mix chicken, mayonnaise, celery, and tarragon with a fork. (I love to add the other ingredients as well: apples, raisins, and walnuts. I've even substituted curry for tarragon, and mandarin oranges for apples.)
3. Serve on a bed of lettuce or sprouts along with crackers or bread sticks. It's also great stuffed in a pita pocket or a croissant.

Yield: Serves 4–6.

Virtual Burgers

Hamburgers and hot dogs are a must on Labor Day, but here's something for the herbivores in the group—these low-fat "burgers."

3–4 potatoes

4 garlic cloves, peeled

Pinch of salt and pepper

1 cup chickpea flour or matzoh meal

1 tablespoon cold water

½ teaspoon turmeric

½ teaspoon ground cumin

½ teaspoon garlic powder

½ teaspoon oregano

2 cups spinach

1 small onion, peeled

2 medium carrots, peeled

3 tablespoons wheat germ

2 tablespoons bulgur wheat

1 large egg, beaten

Vegetable oil for baking pan

Optional toppings

Tomato sauce

Mozzarella cheese, sliced

1. Preheat oven to 375°.
2. Boil potatoes about 45 minutes until soft. Bake peeled garlic cloves in aluminum foil pouch for 45 minutes or until tender. Mash together, adding salt and pepper.
3. In a separate bowl, make a paste of chickpea flour, water, and spices.
4. In a meat grinder or food processor, chop vegetables. In a separate large bowl, combine chopped vegetables, wheat germ, bulgur wheat, and egg. Mix.
5. Add mashed potatoes and chickpea flour to mixture.
6. Form 3½-inch-round patties. Chill 1 hour. Bake on greased pan covered with aluminum foil for 1 hour. Turn over after first ½ hour to brown each side. Raise oven to 400° for last 15 minutes of baking. *Optional*: Add tomato sauce and one slice of cheese to top during last few minutes. Serve in buns, or plain.

Yield: 12 veggie-burgers.

Old-Fashioned Peach Cobbler

This homemade dessert was popular more than one hundred years ago. Juicy peaches are plentiful and ripe in the summer. Or you can substitute apples, blueberries, or cherries for peaches.

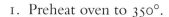

5 large ripe peaches, peeled and sliced	2 teaspoons cinnamon
3 tablespoons maple syrup	¼ teaspoon nutmeg
2 teaspoons lemon juice	⅓ cup unbleached flour, sifted
2 tablespoons water	¼ cup granulated sugar
½ cup light brown sugar	3 tablespoons butter, melted

1. Preheat oven to 350°.
2. In a large mixing bowl, coat peaches with mixture of maple syrup, lemon juice, water, brown sugar, cinnamon, and nutmeg. Put in large baking dish.
3. Mix flour, granulated sugar, and butter together. Crumble over top of peaches.
4. Cover baking dish with aluminum foil. Bake for 30 minutes. Uncover dish and bake additional 10 minutes until crumbs are slightly golden.
5. Serve warm with vanilla ice cream or whipped cream.

Yield: Serves 6–8.

September S'mores

This is a favorite around the campfire. Put a marshmallow, piercing the center, on the tip of a very long tree twig or skewer. Rotate the marshmallow over the grill or fire. Remove when it is toasted. Place on a small chocolate bar between two plain graham crackers. Watch it melt! You will really want "some more!" For a variation, put the gooey melted marshmallow on a chocolate-covered graham cracker smeared with peanut butter.

HALLOWEEN

*H*alloween's origins can be traced back to the time of the Celts—people who lived in the British Isles and France centuries ago. Originally, the Celtic year ended on October 31. Pagans celebrated it as "Samhain," which means "end of summer," and was also the name of the lord of the dead. After October 31 came the period that the ancient Druid priests called "the winter season of death." People wore costumes of animal skins and had large bonfires to ward off spirits and ghosts. When the Romans conquered Great Britain, they added their own customs from a harvest festival on November 1. They honored Pomona, goddess of fruit trees, with offerings of apples and nuts. She is often depicted with a crown of apples. To this day, bobbing for apples is a Halloween game played in the United States, England, Scotland, and Wales.

After Christianity spread in the ninth century, November 1 became All Saints' Day. The evening before, October 31, was called "All Hallows' Even," or "holy evening," and this eventually was condensed to "Halloween." The Celtic customs of honoring the dead, combined with the customs of the harvest, have remained. We dress up as goblins, skeletons, fairies, or witches on flying broomsticks. The Irish, who immigrated to the United States during the 1840s potato famine, carved faces into potatoes and turnips. We turn pumpkins into jack-o'-lanterns with scary faces and devilish grins, lit with candles inside.

Another favorite Halloween tradition is trick-or-treating, which may be traced back to the Irish. Farmers went from house to house, gathering food for the village Halloween celebration. Others say the custom comes from All Souls' Day in England, when people went begging door to door for "a soul-cake, a soulcake, a penny or a soulcake!" (Soulcakes are currant buns.) The practice of giving sweet treats is still a tradition.

HALLOWEEN

Acorn Squash Soup
Black and Orange Pasta
Monster Muffins
Pumpkin Cookies

Halloween Haunted House Party Foods

Frozen ice cubes with plastic bugs inside for punch

Jell-O for slime

Warm spaghetti for worms

Sesame seeds and crushed nuts for insects

Frozen grapes for eyeballs

Bread stuffing for guts

String of hot dogs for intestines

Wet spinach leaves for scary swamp monster gook

Chilled tomato juice or ketchup for blood

Acorn Squash Soup

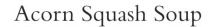

On a cold Halloween night when the wind chills your bones, this soup is perfect to warm your innards. Both pumpkins and acorn squash are abundant during autumn harvests.

2 small acorn squash, halved and seeded,
 or 1 medium pumpkin, seeded and
 cut into wedges
1 carrot, peeled and sliced thin
1 small onion, peeled and chopped
1 tablespoon unsalted butter
4 cups vegetable soup (stock or bouillon)
1 apple, peeled and cut into chunks
1 bay leaf

¼ teaspoon curry
Salt to taste
Pinch of white pepper
½ cup light cream
Pinch of nutmeg or ginger
Chopped fresh parsley or cilantro to garnish
Shredded carrot to garnish
Finely grated Parmesan or
 Gruyère cheese

1. Preheat oven to 400°.
2. Place squash halves or pumpkin wedges facedown in 1 inch of water at the bottom of baking dish. Cover and steam 1 hour until squash skin is tender or pumpkin is soft. Remove from oven. Cool. Scoop squash from the outer rind.
3. While squash or pumpkin is cooking, sauté carrot and onion in butter in a small frying pan until onions are translucent. In a large pot on stove top, add to vegetable stock. *Optional*: If you make your own vegetable stock, boil 4 cups water, 1 whole garlic bulb, peeled, and 8 fresh basil leaves for ½ hour. Strain liquid.
4. To liquid, add apple, bay leaf, curry, salt, and white pepper. Cook over medium heat until apples are soft. Remove bay leaf. Strain.
5. Purée stock mixture in food processor or blender. Return to pot. Add cream, stirring soup over low flame for a few minutes until hot.
6. Pour into a medium scooped-out pumpkin shell. From there, ladle into individual bowls. Sprinkle spice and parsley on top of each serving, and a few shredded carrots for additional orange color. Add cheese if desired.

Yield: Serves 6.

Black and Orange Pasta

Black linguine, dyed with squid ink, can be found in specialty markets. Orange ravioli and tortellini are common in many supermarkets. If pasta is black, decorate platter with sliced carrots. If pasta is orange, then toss in black olives and black sesame seeds.

1 pound pasta (black or orange of your choice)
8 cloves garlic, peeled and minced
1 carrot, peeled and cut into ½-inch rounds, steamed
2–3 tablespoons olive oil
10 black olives and/or 1 tablespoon black sesame seeds
Grated Romano or Parmesan cheese to taste

1. *Black pasta*: In a large pot on stove top, boil pasta in water for about 10 minutes until semisoft. While pasta is boiling, sauté garlic and carrots in olive oil in frying pan. Drain pasta when done. Add sauté to pasta. Mix well. (Garlic will keep away any vampires in the vicinity.)

2. *Orange pasta*: Orange pasta is usually colored with carrot juice or is pumpkin flavored. Boil about 10 minutes. Sauté garlic in olive oil. Put over pasta. Mix gently. Display olives on top. Sprinkle with black sesame seeds. Add grated Romano or Parmesan cheese. Serve to ghoulish guests.

Yield: Serves 6–8 (depending on monstrous appetites!).

Pasta Sauce (Optional)

4 dozen fresh newts en saison sautéed in slime. Stir in boiling cauldron with 1 dodo quill. Add 24 bat's eyes, finely chopped, and a pinch of wart powder (found in specialty sorcery or magic stores). Serve piping hot over black linguine.

*Yield: Serves 1 giant,
3 witches or wizards, or
1 classroom of children.*

Monster Muffins

Muffins

3 cups unbleached flour, sifted

1 teaspoon baking powder

1 teaspoon baking soda

3 large eggs, separated

1 cup granulated sugar

¼ cup vegetable oil

Juice of one lemon

½ cup honey or maple syrup

1 cup strong coffee

1 teaspoon ginger

1 teaspoon cinnamon

1 teaspoon allspice

1 teaspoon cream of tartar

½ cup light raisins

½ cup carrots, peeled and shredded

1 tablespoon shelled almonds, grated

Icing

8 ounces cream cheese

½ cup butter, softened

2 teaspoons vanilla extract

1 pound confectioners' sugar

Red, yellow, and green food coloring

Candy corn, licorice for decorations

1. Preheat oven to 350°.
2. *Muffins*: In a large bowl, sift flour, baking powder, and baking soda together.
3. In another bowl, beat egg yolks and sugar with mixer. Add oil, lemon juice, honey, coffee, and spices. Gradually add flour mixture.
4. In a separate bowl, using clean beaters, beat egg whites with cream of tartar until stiff peaks form. Remove beaters and use rubber spatula to gently fold egg whites, raisins, carrots, and almonds into batter until whites are no longer visible and all ingredients are combined.
5. Insert paper liners into muffin tins. Fill tins ⅔ full to allow muffins to almost double in height. Bake 30 minutes. Cool. Ice.
6. *Orange or green icing*: In a mixing bowl, with an electric mixer, blend cream cheese with butter and vanilla extract. Sift confectioners' sugar. Add to mixture. Blend in 10 drops red and 10 drops yellow food coloring to make orange color (or use carrot juice). Add more if necessary. Or blend in 20 green drops for "monster" icing. Ice muffins with spatula. Put one piece of candy corn or licorice on top of each.

Yield: 2 dozen.

Pumpkin Cookies

These cookies are so-o chewy I wouldn't be surprised if they stayed moist until Thanksgiving! If they last, that is! I had trouble keeping track of how many I made because my family was eating them right out of the oven.

¾ cup butter, softened
6 ounces cream cheese, softened
1 cup light brown sugar
⅔ cup granulated sugar
2 teaspoons vanilla extract
1 large egg, beaten
1 teaspoon nutmeg or mace
¼ teaspoon ginger

1¾ cups pumpkin, canned or cooked
2 cups unbleached flour, sifted
1 teaspoon baking powder
½ cup chopped walnuts
3 tablespoons pitted dates, chopped
12-ounce bag of white-chocolate morsels
Whole blanched almonds or pecan halves
    to decorate each cookie

1. Preheat oven to 375°.
2. In a large bowl, with electric mixer, cream butter, cream cheese, sugars, and vanilla extract. Blend in egg, spices, and pumpkin.
3. Into a separate bowl sift flour and baking powder together. Gradually add to wet mixture.
4. With mixer at low speed, slowly pour in walnuts, dates, and chocolate.
5. When dough is thoroughly mixed, grease cookie sheets or line with parchment. Drop teaspoonfuls of cookie dough on each sheet (about 12–16 will fit). Put one almond or pecan half on top of each cookie. Bake 15–20 minutes. Allow to cool on sheet or rack for 2 minutes. Then lift each cookie with a spatula and place on a plate, in a cookie tin, or in a jar to store until guests come for your Halloween party.

Yield: 9 dozen 2-inch cookies.

THANKSGIVING

$\mathcal{T}$he Pilgrims sailed the *Mayflower* from England to the New World in the summer of 1620 to escape religious persecution. After a perilous two-month voyage, they landed at what is now called Plymouth, Massachusetts. Without homes and food, many starved and died that long, cold winter. The following spring, a member of the Wampanoag tribe named Squanto, who was a long-standing friend of the British explorer named George Weymouth, offered his help. Native Americans taught the Pilgrims how to plant corn, squash, pumpkins, carrots, cabbages, onions, and beans, to hunt deer and wild turkeys, to fish, and to cook what they caught. Oysters and clams were plentiful at the seashore. The settlers ate nuts, berries, grapes, and plums.

The first Thanksgiving was a harvest festival during the fall of 1621 in the Plymouth colony. Governor William Bradford set aside several days of prayer and declared that a harvest feast would be shared by the Pilgrims and Native Americans. During the autumn of 1622, there was no Thanksgiving celebration because the crop was bleak. The following fall, after a season of drought, came rain and rejoicing.

The yearly custom of celebrating Thanksgiving continued wherever the New England Pilgrims settled. A national day of thanksgiving was suggested by the Continental Congress during the American Revolution, but it didn't become a legal holiday until during the Civil War. In 1863, President Abraham Lincoln made Thanksgiving the last Thursday of November. In 1941, an act of Congress changed the day to the fourth Thursday in November, when it is celebrated today. There are parades in various cities, and families get together for a big Thanksgiving meal.

 # THANKSGIVING

Cranberry-Orange Relish

Chestnut Stuffing

Roast Turkey with Potatoes and Carrots

Mushroom Gravy

Pilgrim Pumpkin Pie

Cranberry-Orange Relish

Berries were plentiful for the early settlers. Sasemin *was the Wampanoag tribe's name for "wild cranberry." These bitter berries were used for dyes, healing, and food. The budding flowers of the plant reminded the Pilgrims of the crane, a European bird. Thanksgiving turkey wouldn't be the same without the traditional cranberry sauce or relish. Oranges, sugar, and maple syrup cut the tartness of the cranberry taste.*

12 ounces fresh cranberries

½ cup water

2 teaspoons orange zest

2 tablespoons granulated sugar

1 tablespoon maple syrup

8–10 canned mandarin orange sections

1. Boil cranberries in water with orange zest, sugar, and maple syrup for 10 minutes over medium flame. Stir frequently until liquid boils off and the berries are soft and mushy.
2. Cover pot with lid. Simmer on low flame for another 3–5 minutes.
3. Remove from stove. Put in serving bowl and mix in mandarin oranges. Serve at room temperature.

Yield: Approximately 12 portions.

cranberry flower and bud

Chestnut Stuffing

Italian dried chestnuts are sweet, and sold shelled in many health food stores and gourmet markets. If shelled chestnuts are unavailable, you can roast dark brown chestnuts in the shell. Slit round side of shell with sharp knife—or chestnuts may explode! Bake on a cookie sheet in oven at 400° for about 30 minutes until tender. Scoop out chestnut "meat." I often cook the chestnuts the night before so they are ready to go the next day.

2 cups Italian dried chestnuts, shelled

1 pound challah or white bread, sliced

2 cups boiling water

2 extra large eggs, beaten

Salt and pepper to taste

1 large onion, chopped

2 stalks celery, chopped

2 teaspoons thyme

Vegetable oil for sautéing

1 carrot, shredded

1. Soak chestnuts overnight in 1–2 cups water. The next day, boil chestnuts for around 1½ hours until soft. Chop. Set aside in bowl.
2. Preheat oven to 375°.
3. Place sliced challah or bread in a large bowl. Pour boiling water over challah to soak. Mash with fork until mushy. Add eggs, salt, and pepper. Mix again. Cover with dish towel to keep moist.
4. In a small frying pan, sauté onion, celery, and thyme in oil until onions are soft and translucent (about 5–7 minutes).
5. Uncover challah. Stir in onion-celery mixture with fork. Add chestnuts and shredded carrot for color.
6. Coat bottom of 9-by-12-inch baking dish with oil. Pour in stuffing. Bake 1 hour or until top is golden brown. (I prefer to cook stuffing separately from the turkey, especially if there are vegetarians around.)

Yield: Serves 12.

Roast Turkey with Potatoes and Carrots

Thanksgiving and turkeys go together. One year, my younger son sculpted a tofu turkey for my husband and older son, who are vegetarians. He then proceeded to decorate his "turkey" with black sesame seeds for each eye, a long shred of carrot around the neck, and a slice of Japanese pink ginger underneath the neck. He pushed toothpicks through brussels sprout leaves and attached them to the back for a fan of turkey feathers. After all this work, making a roast turkey seemed quite simple.

14–16-pound turkey
Paprika to taste
Thyme to taste
1 teaspoon white pepper
Salt to taste (optional)
1 tablespoon garlic powder
10 garlic cloves, peeled

20 small red potatoes
3 carrots, peeled and cut into ¾-inch slices

Optional

8 garlic cloves, peeled and softened
1 orange, peeled and sectioned
2 apples, cored and quartered

1. Preheat oven to 400°.
2. Wash turkey and clean out cavity of any pouches containing neck, liver, etc.
3. Sprinkle entire turkey with paprika, thyme, white pepper, salt, and garlic powder. Put 10 garlic cloves in cavity of turkey. Place turkey, legs up, in a very large roasting pan or on a rack in a large pan. Cover with lid or foil to retain juices. Baste every ½ hour or so with a baster.
4. Reduce heat after 1 hour to 350°. Cook about 20 minutes for each pound of meat. The last hour, rotate turkey so legs are on the bottom. Add potatoes and carrots. *Optional*: Smear turkey skin with softened garlic cloves and juice from orange sections. (To soften garlic cloves, slice off top of bulb, and wrap entire bulb in foil. Bake at 400° for about 1 hour until roasted and soft. Squeeze garlic cloves out of husks.) To the bottom of the roasting pan add garlic cloves, apple chunks, and orange sections.
5. Uncover in oven the last 15–20 minutes to roast turkey to a golden brown. (Allow for total roasting time somewhere between 4½–5 hours.)

Yield: Serves 18 or more with no leftovers!

Mushroom Gravy

I like roast turkey plain, but many people can't imagine having turkey without gravy. Here's how to make a tasty gravy.

2–3 cups turkey drippings from roasting pan
½ teaspoon soy or Worcestershire sauce
½ teaspoon thyme
Pinch of salt and pepper

1 tablespoon cornstarch, arrowroot, or flour
1 teaspoon water, room temperature
4 mushrooms, thinly sliced (optional)

1. To reduce fat content, pour the drippings from the pan into a large plastic tub and place on shelf in freezer for 1 hour. Skim off fat.
2. Put "jelled" liquid drippings into pot on stove top. Add soy or Worcestershire sauce, thyme, salt, and pepper.
3. In a separate dish, mix a thin paste of cornstarch and water. One tablespoon will thicken about 2 cups of liquid drippings.
4. Gradually add paste to drippings in pot. Cook over low flame, constantly stirring with a wooden spoon to prevent lumps in gravy.
5. Add mushrooms, if desired, and continue to simmer until they are tender and the gravy is thick. Put sauce in gravy boat. Serve immediately.

Yield: Makes enough for 1 large gravy boat.

Pilgrim Pumpkin Pie

Canned pumpkin is easy to find in the baking goods section of a grocery store, but I always have a left-over pumpkin or two from Halloween on my front steps. They keep until Thanksgiving, since it is cold outside. Scoop out the inside of a medium-size pumpkin, removing seeds (which you can toast and salt later to eat), and boil it on the stove top in a large covered pot with a little hot water until it is soft and stringy. Drain liquid. Since this recipe makes enough filling for two pies, there is a choice between two different types of crusts!

Plain pie crust
½ cup butter or margarine, softened

8 ounces cream cheese, softened

1 teaspoon vanilla extract

¼ teaspoon nutmeg or allspice

1 cup unbleached flour, sifted

Extra flour

Cookie crumb crust
1 cup honey graham cracker crumbs

3 tablespoons ground walnuts

¼ cup confectioners' sugar

3 tablespoons butter, melted

2 tablespoons maple syrup

Filling
2 cups pumpkin, canned or cooked

1⅓ cups evaporated milk

3 heaping tablespoons dark brown sugar

4 tablespoons granulated sugar

2 tablespoons molasses

1 teaspoon vanilla extract

Pinch of orange zest (optional)

1 teaspoon cinnamon

½ teaspoon ginger

¼ teaspoon ground cloves

⅛ teaspoon nutmeg or mace

2 eggs, separated

1 teaspoon cream of tartar

5 pecan halves

1. Preheat oven to 350°.

2. *Plain crust*: In a bowl cream butter and cream cheese with an electric mixer. Add vanilla and nutmeg. Gradually add flour. Remove from bowl and knead into a large ball. Dust with flour if it is sticky. With a rolling pin, roll out crust ¼-inch thick on floured surface. Lift up dough and place in pie pan. Pinch dough around the edge of pan and cut off excess. One trick to remember, so the pie crust doesn't shrink, is to put another smaller pan on top of the crust and bake 5–7 minutes. Cool a few minutes. Remove small pan, then fill crust.

3. *Cookie crumb crust*: Mix cookie crumbs and walnuts with confectioners' sugar. Melt butter and stir into mixture with maple syrup. Press mixture into pie pan to form crust by smoothing edges with fingers dipped in water. Then fill.

4. *Filling*: By hand or with an electric mixer, combine pumpkin, evaporated milk, both sugars, molasses, vanilla extract, orange zest, and spices into large mixing bowl.

5. Separate egg yolks from egg whites and discard one yolk. Beat remaining yolk and add it to the pumpkin filling.

6. In another bowl, beat both egg whites with cream of tartar until stiff peaks form. With a spatula, fold fluffy egg whites into batter until thoroughly mixed. Pour filling into both crusts. Make a flower pattern on top of pie with 5 pecan halves.

7. Bake 45 minutes to an hour until pie puffs up and is an autumn orange-brown color.

8. Serve warm or chilled with a dollop of whipped cream, a pinch of nutmeg or cinnamon, or vanilla or maple walnut ice cream.

Yield: 2 9-inch pies.

CHANUKAH

Chanukah falls between late November and December, depending on the Jewish calendar, and lasts eight days. The holiday, also called "The Festival of Lights," celebrates the Maccabee warriors' victory over the forces of the Syrian king Antiochus IV, a tyrant who wanted the Israelites to worship many idols instead of their own one God. Some Jewish people obeyed the king's orders, either out of fear or because they liked the Greek way of life and no longer wanted to be different. Others became angry, like Judah Maccabee, and fought back. Judah's determination, strength, and bravery inspired other Jews to join him in his rebellion against the king. Although the Jews were fewer in number, they were fierce in their belief. Eventually they won, driving out Antiochus's army. In Hebrew, *Maccabee* means "hammer."

The triumphant Maccabees returned to the Temple in Jerusalem and found it ruined after years of war. They rebuilt it and erected a new altar with a candelabrum. There was only enough oil to burn for one day during their "Feast of Dedication" (*Chanukah* means "dedication"), but a great miracle happened: The lamp burned for eight days! To commemorate the eight days of life, a candle is lit on a menorah (also called a *chanukiah* or *hannukiah*) for each of the eight nights. During the holiday, Jews are reminded of how Judaism has survived for over two thousand years, throughout many hard times in history.

Foods fried in oil, such as potato pancakes (*latkes*) and jelly doughnuts (*sufganiyot*), are eaten during this holiday as further reminders of the miraculous event.

CHANUKAH

Pearl's Potato Latkes
Avi's Cinnamon-Stick Applesauce
Bubbe's Baked Apples
Uncle Solly's Sufganiyot/Jelly Doughnuts

Pearl's Potato Latkes

Ashkenazi Jews, whose ancestors came from eastern Europe, eat potato pancakes, or latkes, to celebrate Chanukah. When I was eight years old, I ate so many latkes I felt as if I had swallowed a bowling ball!

5 large potatoes, peeled
1 medium onion, peeled
2 large eggs, beaten

¼ cup matzoh meal
Salt and pepper to taste
Vegetable oil for frying

1. Grate peeled potatoes and onion by hand or in food processor. In a large bowl, combine eggs, potatoes, and onion.
2. Blend in matzoh meal, salt, and pepper.
3. In a large frying pan over a medium flame, heat 1-inch layer of oil. Drop in 1 heaping tablespoon of mixture for each latke. A few latkes (about 5) can cook at a time. Turn over when crisp and golden.
4. Drain on double layer of paper towels over a thick paper shopping bag.
5. Serve piping hot with sour cream or applesauce.
6. *Cajun latkes:* Add a pinch of cayenne pepper or a chopped jalapeño. Serve with a *sweet salsa* on the side: Mix together 3 kiwi fruits or a large peach, peeled and finely chopped, a small red onion, peeled and chopped, a handful of chopped cilantro, and apple cider vinegar to taste.

Yield: 16–18 latkes, approximately 3 inches round.

Avi's Cinnamon-Stick Applesauce

A spoonful of chunky applesauce is a must with latkes.

8 large McIntosh apples	¼ cup dark raisins
½ cup maple syrup	1 large lemon, quartered
2–3 cinnamon sticks	Dark brown sugar to taste

1. In a large pot, place whole apples. Pour maple syrup over apples.
2. Add cinnamon sticks, raisins, and lemon wedges to pot. Sprinkle brown sugar on top of apples. Partially cover and simmer until apples are soft and runny.
3. Scoop apples from skins, discarding skins—or eat them, they are full of vitamins. Mash apples through strainer or sieve into a bowl.

Yield: Serves 12 (depending on the size of the dollops of sauce).

Bubbe's Baked Apples

If you prefer baked apples like Grandma's, Rome apples are the best. Preheat oven to 375°. Place cored apples in large glass baking dish. Stuff each center with brown sugar, cinnamon, raisins, and walnuts (optional) to taste. Squeeze juice from one lemon over apples, placing lemon wedges around the pan. Pour ½ cup of maple syrup over apples. Fill bottom of pan with ½ inch of water. Bake 45 minutes or until the apples are firm on the outside, soft in the center, with the raisins chewy and the skins caramelized like candy from the sugar.

Uncle Solly's Sufganiyot/Jelly Doughnuts

Sephardic Jews, for the most part, are descendants of Jews from Spain, Portugal, Italy, and the Middle East. Some come from as far as Northern Africa and India! A traditional Chanukah treat from their tradition is jelly doughnuts, called sufganiyot (SOOF-gahn-nee-oht).

1 package active dry yeast
1 teaspoon granulated sugar (for yeast)
¼ cup warm water (105°–115°F)
1¾ cups milk
½ cup butter
1 large egg, beaten
¾ cup granulated sugar
3 dashes salt

¼ teaspoon nutmeg
1 teaspoon cinnamon
Rind of 1 small lemon, finely grated
5½ cups unbleached flour, sifted
Grape, raspberry, or strawberry jelly, jam,
   or preserves
Vegetable oil for frying
Confectioners' sugar

1. In a small bowl, dissolve yeast and 1 teaspoon of sugar in warm water for 10 minutes.
2. Scald milk in a small saucepan on stove top. Add butter to hot milk. Continue to heat, stirring constantly, until butter is melted. Remove from heat.
3. When milk and butter mixture is lukewarm, put in large mixing bowl. With an electric mixer, mix in egg, ¾ cup of sugar, salt, nutmeg, cinnamon, lemon rind, and yeast mixture. Gradually add flour. Knead until elastic ball of dough forms. Cover with dish towel. Set aside in warm area. Allow dough to double in size. Punch down after about 2 hours.
4. Tear off pieces of dough into plum-size balls. With a rolling pin, flatten each ball into a pancake. Put ½ teaspoon of jelly in center of a pancake. Place a plain pancake on top. Seal edges with room-temperature water.
5. *For a doughnut hole:* Tear off dough and roll into small walnut-size balls. Pierce center of each ball with a skewer or knife. Stuff ¼ teaspoon of jelly inside each ball. Smooth dough over with water to seal hole.
6. In a large pot, heat enough oil to deep-fry dough. When oil is bubbling, pop a few doughnuts (or holes) in at a time. Deep-fry about 3 minutes, rolling dough around with a ladle until lightly brown. Drain on paper towels on a plate. Replace towels when greasy.

7. Sprinkle confectioners' sugar on top of doughnuts. For holes, put confectioners' sugar (about ½ cup at a time) in a paper lunch bag. Drop a few nuggets at a time into the bag and shake until dusted.

Yield: About 2 dozen doughnuts or 3 dozen doughnut holes (as long as you don't eat them while you're making them!).

KWANZAA

*K*wanzaa was created in 1966 by Dr. Maulana Karenga as an African-American holiday based on African harvest festivals. *Kwanzaa* means "first fruits" in one African language, Swahili. It is celebrated for seven nights, from December 26 to January 1. A seven-branched candleholder (*kinara*) is lit with candles representing the seven principles: a black candle for the center, signifying the African people; three red candles on the left side representing struggle; and three green ones on the right symbolizing the hills of Africa, hopes, and dreams.

The Seven Principles

Umoja (oo-MOH-jah): unity
Kujichagulia (koo-jee-chah-goo-LEE-ah): self-determination
Ujima (oo-JEE-mah): collective work and responsibility
Ujamaa (oo-jah-MAH): cooperative economics
Nia (NEE-ah): purpose
Kuumba (koo-OOM-bah): creativity
Imani (ee-MAH-nee): faith

Everyone in the family drinks from a unity cup (*kikombe cha umoja*) on the special feast day (*Karamu*). A handmade straw mat (*mkeka*) is placed on the table. A basket is filled with fresh fruit and ears of corn (*muhindi*). The kernels represent the children, and the stalk, the father. Everyone sings, dances, tells stories, brings little gifts (like African dolls, drums, books on culture), wears the black, red, and green colors of African dress, and eats delicious meals celebrating the spirit of Kwanzaa.

KWANZAA

Buttermilk Corn Bread
Sweet Potato Pudding
Baked Chicken Nuggets
Black-Eyed Pea Cutlets and Collard Greens

▼▼▼▼▼▼▼▼▼▼

Buttermilk Corn Bread

Corn symbolizes the harvest. Many people place one ear of corn for each child in the family in a bowl on the table. In this recipe, add red chili pepper to represent the red candles lit in the kinara *(candle-holder), and jalapeño peppers for the green candles. The red and green peppers dot the yellow corn bread in a colorful way.*

1 cup yellow cornmeal

1 cup unbleached flour, sifted

¼ cup granulated sugar

3 teaspoons baking powder

½ teaspoon salt (optional)

¼ cup butter, softened

1 cup buttermilk or plain milk

1 extra large egg, beaten

1 teaspoon orange zest

1 small jalapeño pepper, diced

½ teaspoon red chili pepper, finely chopped

Canola or corn oil for greasing pan

1. Preheat oven to 400°.
2. By hand or with an electric mixer, mix cornmeal, flour, sugar, baking powder, and salt in bowl. Set aside.
3. In a separate bowl, with a mixer, blend together butter, milk, egg, orange zest, and jalapeño and red chili peppers. Add dry ingredients to wet, and mix with a few quick turns.
4. Bake in a greased 9-by-9-inch pan for 30 minutes. Cut into 3-inch squares. Serve warm.

   Yield: 9 squares.

Sweet Potato Pudding

Sweet potato pie is often served on Kwanzaa, so feel free to put this pudding into a pie crust and bake.

4 large sweet potatoes	¼ teaspoon allspice
2 sweet apples, peeled and cut into chunks	¼ teaspoon cinnamon
½ cup pineapple chunks	1 teaspoon ginger
1 tablespoon maple syrup	8 large walnuts, shelled
¼ teaspoon nutmeg	2 pats of butter

1. Preheat oven to 350°.
2. Boil sweet potatoes in large covered pot about 1 hour or until tender. Remove. Cool. Peel. Mash in large bowl with a fork, or in mixer.
3. Gently stir together apples, pineapple, maple syrup, and spices. Fold into sweet potato mixture with spatula.
4. Pour mixture into approximately 7½-by-12-inch baking dish. Smooth surface with spatula. Dot with walnuts and butter. Cover pan with aluminum foil to prevent drying. Bake 1 hour.
5. Remove foil from pudding last 15 minutes. Serve steaming hot.

Yield: Serves 10–12.

Baked Chicken Nuggets

I find baking the chicken healthier than frying. It uses less oil and doesn't splatter grease on top of the stove. If a lot of people are celebrating the holiday together, bite-size pieces are perfect for appetizers dipped into a sauce of your choice, or served just plain. For dinner, I like them with mashed potatoes and gravy, warm biscuits, and a piece of buttered corn. Mmm!

6 chicken cutlets
   (boneless, skinless breasts, about 3½ pounds)
2 cups bread crumbs or flour
Salt and pepper to taste

1 teaspoon fresh parsley, finely chopped
2 extra large eggs, beaten
Vegetable oil to grease pan
Sandwich-size paper bag

1. Preheat oven to 400°.
2. Wash cutlets in cold water. Cut into bite-size pieces.
3. Mix bread crumbs or flour—whichever coating you choose—with salt, pepper, and parsley. Put ½ cup at a time inside a paper bag. (Refill bag as you coat more pieces.)
4. First dip each nugget into a small bowl with beaten eggs. Drop a few nuggets at a time into the bag. Holding the top of bag, shake, making sure each nugget is coated. Remove nuggets from bag. Repeat until all the chicken is coated.
5. Place in greased baking dish. Put in oven for about 7 minutes. Flip over and bake for another 7 minutes or until golden brown.

   Yield: Serves 10 people for hors d'oeuvres, about 6 people as a meal.

This is about a 1¼"
bite-size chicken piece.

Black-Eyed Pea Cutlets and Collard Greens

Chickpea flour can be bought in many health food stores.

1 cup black-eyed peas, cooked or canned
1 cup chickpea flour
1 teaspoon garlic powder
¼ teaspoon cayenne pepper
1 teaspoon ground cumin
1½ cups water
⅓ cup fresh cilantro, chopped

1 medium onion, peeled and grated
Vegetable oil
1 pound collard greens
1 red onion
6 garlic cloves, peeled, or ½ teaspoon garlic powder
Salt and pepper to taste

1. *Black-eyed pea cutlets*: In a large bowl or food processor, mash black-eyed peas. Mix in flour and spices to make a paste. Add water and cilantro. Mix in onion by hand, or with a quick turn in the food processor. Shape into cutlets before cooking.

2. *For low-fat cooking*: Preheat oven to 400°. Coat large baking dish with oil and bake mixture about 5 minutes on each side or until golden brown.

3. *For frying*: Over a medium flame, heat an inch of oil in frying pan. Using a large serving spoon, drop mixture into pan. Fry on both sides about 3 minutes or until golden brown. *To drain*: Put cutlets on a large paper grocery bag with a few layers of paper towels on top to absorb the grease. Serve immediately, or reheat when guests arrive.

4. *Collard greens*: Steam or boil 1 pound collard greens 10 minutes or until leaves are tender. Drain. Cut into small pieces. Peel and chop ½ cup red onion and mash 6 garlic cloves. In separate large frying pan, sauté onions, garlic (or ½ teaspoon garlic powder), salt, and pepper in oil until onions and garlic are soft. Stir in greens and sauté for an additional 5 minutes.

Yield: 18 cutlets, about 3½ inches in diameter.

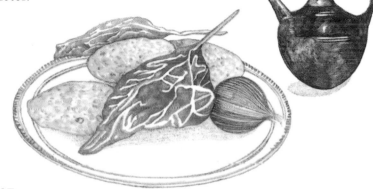

 # CHRISTMAS

Christmas marks the Nativity, or the birth of Jesus in a stable in Bethlehem. Christians throughout the world observe the holiday on December 25. Christmas Eve has also become a time when family and friends get together and bake favorite desserts for the Christmas meal the next day; trim the Christmas tree with tinsel, lights, and trinkets collected over the years; go caroling; and attend a midnight mass, where beautiful hymns are sung. The modern Christmas tree tradition began in Germany around the seventeenth century, spread from there to France, then to England in 1841; from there it came to America with immigrants. Dutch settlers brought Sinterklass, a precursor of Santa Claus, to the New World. The patron saint St. Nicholas was the bishop of Myra, an ancient seaport city in Asia Minor. He gave gifts to the poor, especially children. The "St. Nick" we know is a jolly, white-bearded, red-suited fellow from the North Pole who delivers presents to children all over the world on Christmas Eve. The following day is a merry time of sharing gifts from under the tree and a big family meal.

Long before Jesus, midwinter festivals were celebrated by many cultures. During their holiday of Saturnalia, the Romans fastened candles to trees to light up the winter. The customs of hanging mistletoe over an entranceway, displaying wreaths on front doors, decorating homes with holly branches and evergreen boughs, burning Yule logs, and toasting from wassail bowls are believed to come from pre-Christian Germanic, Druid, and Celtic rites for the winter solstice. They bring warmth and joy inside as the days grow long and dark outside.

CHRISTMAS

Santa's Elves' Eggless Eggnog
Mulled Apple Cider
Candy Cane Hot Chocolate
Spiced and Iced Gingerbread Animals
Yuletide Date Logs and Snowballs
Christmas Cranberry-Apple Tea Loaf
Mrs. Claus's Plum Pudding

Santa's Elves' Eggless Eggnog

Santa's elves have been watching out for his health and cholesterol count all year, so there are no eggs in this eggnog. Last Christmas all the reindeer complained that the sleigh was too heavy to pull—and it wasn't the size of the presents! Santa also nearly got stuck down the old chimney. But even though this is a healthier version of the traditional recipe, Santa wouldn't let Mrs. Claus take out the cream. "Or else," he said, "I might as well be drinking yogurt!" Mrs. Claus shot back with, "Not such a bad idea, you red-vested sweetie!"

1½ cups evaporated milk	1 cup heavy cream
6 teaspoons granulated sugar	Pinch of nutmeg or mace
1 teaspoon vanilla extract	Cracked ice or ice cubes

1. Put evaporated milk, sugar, and vanilla in blender. Whip 2 minutes. Set aside.
2. Use whisk or electric mixer to whip heavy cream until peaks form. Fold into evaporated milk mixture.
3. Sprinkle with nutmeg or mace (they come from the same fruit). Serve chilled with cracked ice or ice cubes.

   Yield: Serves 4 (double recipe as needed for a large punch bowl).

Mulled Apple Cider

"Mulled" means to heat, sweeten, and flavor with spices for drinking. The origin of this drink is uncertain, but a spiced ale or punch called "wassail" was used to toast one's health in England on Christmas Eve and on the Twelfth Night of Christmas, going back to medieval and Shakespearean times. It is believed that the Wise Men followed a star in the sky to where Jesus was born in Bethlehem, arriving twelve days after his birth. That is why many people begin the holiday on Christmas Eve and end it with Epiphany, or the Twelfth Night. While you're trimming the tree, this hot drink will warm your insides from head to toe. Close your eyes and inhale the wonderful aroma.

2 quarts apple cider	½ teaspoon allspice
10 whole cloves	Peel of half an orange
4 cinnamon sticks	Pinch of nutmeg or mace

1. In a large pot, simmer (do not boil) all ingredients.
2. After cider has steamed, strain out cloves and orange peel.
3. Pour into mugs or punch glasses, and serve hot with a bit of a cinnamon stick.

Yield: Serves 8.

Candy Cane Hot Chocolate

Imagine the wind blowing outside. Windowpanes are feathered with crystal patterns of ice. You're bundled under a warm quilt on a thick woolen rug in front of the fireplace with your sister, brother, or cousins. As you cuddle, hoping for Santa to fly over the roof with his trusty reindeer, you hear something. Is that a jingle in the air? Icicles cracking as a sleigh touches the shingles? Take a sip while you're waiting. And if you want to, add a pinch of cinnamon on the froth!

Ingredients to have on hand
Boiling water
Cocoa powder
Honey or granulated sugar
Low-fat milk
Marshmallows
Candy canes or peppermint sticks

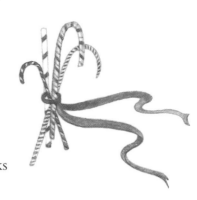

1. Fill a teapot with water and boil.
2. For every mug of milk, use 1 heaping teaspoon of cocoa. Put cocoa in mug. Dissolve with 1 teaspoon of boiling water. Add 1 teaspoon of honey or sugar to mug. Mix with spoon, creating a paste.
3. In a large pot, scald milk until frothy and foaming. Add to mug of cocoa mixture. Stir well, adding a marshmallow, a small candy cane, or a peppermint stick. Serve steaming.

Yield: Make as many mugs as there are people.

Spiced and Iced Gingerbread Animals

Gingerbread can be used to build houses, or make animals, people, or musical instruments—whatever shape you choose. I've collected several kinds of metal and plastic cookie-cutter forms over the years for many occasions. Animal shapes are nice in a diorama of a manger or for decorating the Christmas tree. If you do use them for tree decorations, make a small hole (about ¼ inch in diameter) at the top of each raw cookie—large enough to slip a thin red silk ribbon or gold thread through—so you can hang the cookie after it has cooled. Another great use for gingerbread is as a snack for Santa when he comes down the chimney to leave gifts. Don't forget the glass of milk!

5–6 tablespoons butter
½ cup dark brown sugar
1 large egg, beaten
½ cup dark molasses
¼ cup water
3 cups unbleached flour, sifted

1 teaspoon baking soda
¼ teaspoon ground cloves
¼ teaspoon nutmeg
½ teaspoon cinnamon
1 teaspoon ginger
Extra flour

Raisins, Red Hots for decoration

1. In a bowl with an electric mixer, cream butter, sugar, egg, and molasses. Gradually add water until smooth.

2. In a separate large mixing bowl, sift flour, baking soda, and spices. Gradually add to butter mixture.

3. Dust fingers with flour and divide cookie dough into two balls. Roll out dough with rolling pin on floured surface to about $\frac{3}{16}$-inch thickness. Press cookie cutters into sheet of dough. Save excess dough and reuse to form another ball. Repeat this process until all dough is used.

4. Preheat oven to 350° while decorating cookies.

5. Line cookie sheets with parchment paper or use greased or nonstick pans. Decorate cookies with raisins, Red Hots, or leave plain. Bake 8 minutes (and no more!) until doubled in thickness. Cool on rack.

6. *Icing:* Make a paste of 1 cup confectioners' sugar, 1 teaspoon water, lemon juice to taste, and a pinch of cinnamon. Decorate cookies with a small paintbrush *after* cookies have cooled.

Yield: 4½ dozen (depending on size and shape of form).

Yuletide Date Logs and Snowballs

Gather a group of friends to roll these logs and snowballs for a no-bake dessert!

2 cups pitted dates, chopped
½ cup water
1 pat butter or margarine

Shredded coconut for rolling
Blanched whole almonds
Grated walnuts or almonds

roll mixture inside wax paper

coconut flakes
date nut mixture

1. In small pot on stove top, stir chopped dates, water, and butter over low flame for 4 minutes to create a mushy paste. Chill mixture ½ hour in refrigerator to harden slightly.

2. *Logs:* Coat wax paper or foil (about 8 by 12 inches) with a 2-inch-wide strip of coconut. Add date mixture on top of coconut layer, and roll lengthwise into tight ropelike strand (about ¾-inch thick), gently squeezing the date log as you coat and roll (see diagram). Chill overnight. Cut long "log" into smaller 1¼-inch logs. Put a whole almond on top center of each log.

3. *Snowballs:* This method is easier. Roll date mixture into 1-inch-round balls. (Dip fingertips into bowl of cold water to smooth balls.) Dip date ball into grated nuts, and then into shredded coconut, coating entire "snowball." Insert whole almond or place on top center of each ball. Chill several hours, or serve at room temperature.

Yield: About 2 dozen.

Christmas Cranberry-Apple Tea Loaf

Cranberries are so festive during this time of year. If there are any left after trimming the tree, this bread is scrumptious on Christmas morning. It can also be enjoyed throughout the winter season.

1 cup fresh cranberries

1 cup chopped walnuts (optional)

2 tablespoons orange zest

1 large apple, peeled and chopped

1 extra large egg, beaten

1 teaspoon vanilla extract

2 tablespoons butter, melted

¾ cup orange juice

1 cup granulated sugar

2 cups unbleached flour, sifted

1 teaspoon baking powder

1 teaspoon baking soda

1. Preheat oven to 350°.
2. Mix cranberries, walnuts, orange zest, and apple in small bowl. Set aside.
3. In another bowl, beat egg with mixer until frothy. Continue to mix, adding vanilla, butter, orange juice, and sugar.
4. Sift together flour, baking powder, and baking soda.
5. With mixer gradually add dry ingredients to wet. Blend until smooth. Stir in the cranberry-apple-nut mixture.
6. Pour batter into 4½-by-13-inch greased bread pan (or 2 smaller bread pans). Bake 1 hour or until top of bread splits slightly. Test with toothpick. (Insert in center as deep as possible, and remove. If the toothpick is dry, the bread is done.)

Yield: 1 long loaf or 2 small loaves.

Mrs. Claus's Plum Pudding

Once again, Mrs. Claus showed love and concern for her husband. "Can't you eat a nice bowl of fruit? Strawberries and kiwis are red and green." The elves nodded in agreement, but Santa's eyes twinkled as he begged for a sweeter dessert. Naturally, Mrs. Claus caved in when he chortled, "My dear Mrs. Claus, it's Christmastime! A little plum pudding never hurt anyone." "Plum pudding doesn't have plums in it!" she said. To which he replied, "Well, but it's a fruitcake!"

2–3 cups plain bread crumbs

1½ teaspoons cinnamon

½ teaspoon ground cloves

½ teaspoon allspice

½ teaspoon nutmeg

¼ teaspoon ginger

¾ cup milk, scalded

½ cup currants

½ cup dark raisins

½ cup light raisins

½ cup candied citron, chopped

½ cup candied cherries, chopped

½ cup orange peel, finely chopped

½ cup pitted dates, chopped

½ cup almonds or pecans, chopped

½ cup apple cider

Juice and grated rind of one lemon

½ cup butter, softened

¾ cup light brown sugar

3 extra large eggs, beaten

1 cup flour, sifted

1 cup molasses

1. In small bowl, mix bread crumbs and spices. Add milk. Set aside.
2. In a large bowl, toss fruits and nuts. Soak in cider and lemon juice.
3. In a separate bowl, cream butter and sugar. Add eggs. Gradually mix in flour, then molasses.
4. By hand, combine all mixtures. Pour into greased molds, ⅔ full, and cover with foil.
5. Place on rack or steamer inside a large covered pot filled with about 2 inches of water. Steam on stove top about 5 hours, depending on size of the molds. Add water as necessary to bottom of pot while steaming. Remove pudding from molds. Serve hot.

Yield: 2 molds (serves about 24 elves or 12 people).

Note: To store, keep moist in sealed tin, and steam again ½ hour before serving. Or serve immediately with *chilled hard sauce*. There are many kinds of hard sauces. Santa likes a cream cheese and lemon one that he puts on his hot plum pudding: Cream 4 ounces cream cheese with 2 cups confectioners' sugar (add more for desired consistency). Mix in 1 teaspoon lemon zest, 1 teaspoon vanilla extract, and a pinch of nutmeg and cinnamon. Chill 1 hour.

GLOSSARY

BAKE: to cook in an oven

BEAT: to stir repeatedly until mixed

BLANCH: to cover with boiling water until food is easy to peel

BOIL: to cook in liquid until bubbles rise to the surface

BROIL: to cook under or over direct heat

BROWN: to sear meat on both sides by dry pan frying quickly to retain juices and taste

CARAMELIZE: to burn natural or added sugar to color or flavor food

CHILL: to cool moderately

CHOP: to cut into pieces

CHUNK: to cut into cubes

COAT: to cover with a layer (e.g., coating with bread crumbs)

CREAM: to blend ingredients with electric mixer until softened

DASH: less than ⅛ teaspoon (in liquid measure, about 8 drops)

DICE: to cut into tiny cubes about ¼-inch in size

DOLLOP: a heaping spoonful, or lump

DRAIN: to take away excess liquid

DUST: to coat lightly

FLUFF: to add air to

FOLD: to turn gently onto itself (e.g., folding egg whites into a mixture)

FRY: to cook in hot fat or oil

GARNISH: to decorate

GLAZE: to coat with a transparent liquid

GRATE: to grind or shred into very small pieces

GREASE: to coat with butter, margarine, or oil (as in greasing pans)

GRIND: to crush into very fine pieces

KNEAD: to mix by folding, pressing, and squeezing

LADLE: to transfer liquid by means of a deep spoon

MARINADE: a liquid used to flavor by soaking before cooking

MASH: to crush and mix a food (often with a fork) into a soft mass

MINCE: to chop into very fine pieces

MIX: to combine ingredients

MOLD: a hollow form

PARCHMENT PAPER: a liner for cookie sheets for baking

PEAK: a conical point formed when mixture (e.g., egg whites) stiffens

PICKLE: to marinate in spices and brine

PINCH: a small amount held between thumb and forefinger (less than a dash)

PURÉE: to blend to a smooth consistency

QUICHE PAN: a utensil with removable side and bottom

ROAST: to cook by dry heat, as in an oven or on a spit

SAUTÉ: to cook in a small amount of fat (butter, margarine, or oil)

SCALD: to heat liquid (usually milk) just below the boiling point

SEASON: to flavor (as in seasoning meat)

SHRED: to cut into very thin strips

SIFT: to pass through a sieve

SIMMER: to cook slowly on a moderately low flame

SKEWER: to pierce with a stick or other sharp object

SPATULA: a flat utensil of metal (used for lifting and flipping) or rubber (used for gently folding or mixing)

SPRIG: a little twig with leaves

SPRINKLE: to scatter drops or particles lightly

STEAMER: a utensil used to cook over boiling water without allowing the water to touch the food

TENDER: soft in texture

TRANSLUCENT: letting light show through, but not clear

WHISK: a wire utensil used for beating

ZEST: grated orange or lemon peel

Additional Notes: Differences in Ingredients

CONFECTIONERS' SUGAR VERSUS GRANULATED SUGAR: Confectioners' sugar is a fine powder, while granulated sugar is grains of sugar.

BAKING SODA VERSUS BAKING POWDER: Baking soda is sodium bicarbonate, and baking powder is sodium bicarbonate with salt and cream of tartar.

DARK CORN SYRUP VERSUS LIGHT CORN SYRUP: Dark corn syrup has a more robust flavor than light syrup.

MARGARINE VERSUS BUTTER: Margarine is a vegetable-based product, and butter is derived from milk.

INDEX

A

Acorn Squash Soup, 74
Apple Cider, Mulled, 101
Apple-and-Walnut Ḥaroset, 42
apple(s)
  and Walnut Ḥaroset, 42
  Bubbe's Baked, 89
  Cinnamon-Stick Applesauce, 89
  Cranberry Tea Loaf, 105
  Mulled Cider, 101
  Sweet Potato Pudding, 95
  Waldorf Salad, 52
Applesauce, Avi's Cinnamon-Stick,
  89

B

Baked Chicken Nuggets, 96
Banana Bread, Laid-Back, 68
beans
  Black-Eyed Pea Cutlets, 97
  Stars and Stripes Fusilli, 63
  Three-Bean Chili and Guacamole,
    14
beef
  Classic Brisket, 44
  Corned, and Cabbage, 27
  Sweet and Sour Meatballs, 54
Belgian Waffles, 58
beverages
  Candy Cane Hot Chocolate, 102
  Jack Frost's Tropical Punch, 12
  Mulled Apple Cider, 101
  Papa's Lemonade, 59
  Santa's Elves' Eggless Eggnog, 100
Black and Orange Pasta, 75
Black-Eyed Pea Cutlets and Collard
  Greens, 97
Blueberry Pancakes, 58
bread(s)/rolls
  Buttermilk Corn Bread, 94
  Chestnut Stuffing, 81
  Cranberry-Apple Tea Loaf, 105

Fluffy Cinnamon French Toast, 48
Hot Cross Breakfast Buns, 36
Irish Soda Bread, 25
Laid-Back Banana Bread, 68
Monster Muffins, 76
Potato Crescent Horns, 12-13
Sufganiyot/Jelly Doughnuts, 90-91
Buttermilk Corn Bread, 94

C

cabbage
  Corned Beef and, 27
  in Waldorf Salad, 52
cake(s)
  Cupid Cupcakes, 20
  Flourless Chocolate, Fanny's, 45
  Lemon Poppy Pound, 31
  Mrs. Claus's Plum Pudding, 106
candy
  Cane Hot Chocolate, 102
  Chocolate-Lover's Lollipops, 19
  Mama's Mocha Truffles, 48
  September S'mores, 71
Cheesecake, Patriotic, 64
Chestnut Stuffing, 81
chicken
  Easy Salad, 69
  Nuggets, Baked, 96
Chocolate Chip Cookies, 59
Chocolate-Dipped Strawberries, 49
Chocolate-Lover's Lollipops, 19
Cinnamon-Stick Applesauce, Avi's,
  89
Classic Brisket, 44
coconut
  in Date Logs and Snowballs, 104
Collard Greens, Black-Eyed Pea
  Cutlets and, 97
cookies
  Chocolate Chip, 59
  Gingerbread Animals, 103
  Heart-Shaped Sugar, 18

Oatmeal Raisin "Ant," 30
Pumpkin, 77
Corn Bread, Buttermilk, 94
Corned Beef and Cabbage,
  27
Cranberry-Apple Tea Loaf,
  Christmas, 105
Cranberry-Orange Relish, 80
Cucumber, Yogurt, and Mint Salad,
  52
Cupid Cupcakes, 20

D

Date Logs and Snowballs, Yuletide,
  104
Date-and-Almond Ḥaroset, 42
desserts. *See also* cake(s); candy;
  cookies; fruit; pies
  Christmas Cranberry-Apple Tea
    Loaf, 105
  Monster Muffins, 76
  Patriotic Cheesecake, 64
  Sweet Potato Pudding, 95
  Yuletide Date Logs and Snowballs,
    104
Doughnuts, Uncle Solly's Jelly,
  90-91

E

Easter eggs, decorating, 34
Easy Chicken Salad, 69
Eggnog, Santa's Elves' Eggless, 100
eggs
  Chopped Egg Salad, 35
  decorating Easter, 34
  Quarterback Quiche, 15

F

Firecracker Potato Salad, 62
Flourless Chocolate Cake, Fanny's,
  45
French Toast, Fluffy Cinnamon, 48

frostings/icings
  Pink Frosting, 21
  for Gingerbread Animals, 103
  for Monster Muffins, 76
fruit
  All-American Fruit Salad, 65
  Apple-and-Walnut Haroset, 42
  Blueberry Pancakes, 58
  Bubbe's Baked Apples, 89
  Chocolate-Dipped Strawberries,
    49
  Cinnamon-Stick Applesauce, 89
  Cranberry-Orange Relish, 80
  Date-and-Almond Haroset, 42
  Mrs. Claus's Plum Pudding, 106
  Old-Fashioned Peach Cobbler, 71

G
Gingerbread Animals, 103
glossary, 108-109
Gravy, Mushroom, 83
Guacamole, Three-Bean Chili and,
  14

H
Halloween Haunted House Party
    Foods, 73
harosets, 42
Heart-Shaped Sugar Cookies, 18
Hot Chocolate, Candy Cane, 102
Hot Cross Breakfast Buns, 36

I
Irish Soda Bread, 25

L
Lamb, Sunday Roast, 37
Lemon Poppy Pound Cake, 31
Lemonade, Papa's, 59
Lucky Clover Salad, 24

M
Matzoh Ball Soup, Vegetarian, 43
Meatballs, Sweet and Sour, 54
Middle Eastern dishes
  Cucumber, Yogurt, and Mint Salad,
    52
  Orange Couscous, 53
  Wild Rice Pilaf, 53
Mocha Truffles, Mama's, 48
Molly's Potato and Barley Soup, 26
Muffins, Monster, 76
Mushroom Gravy, 83

O
Oatmeal Raisin "Ant" Cookies, 30
Orange Couscous, 53

P
pancakes
  Blueberry, 58
  Pearl's Potato Latkes, 88
pasta
  Black and Orange, 75
  Orange Couscous, 53
  Stars and Stripes Fusilli, 63
Patriotic Cheesecake, 64
Peach Cobbler, Old-Fashioned, 71
pies
  Pilgrim Pumpkin, 84-85
  Quarterback Quiche, 15
  Sweet Potato, 95
Pink Frosting, 21
Plum Pudding, Mrs. Claus's, 106
Potato Crescent Horns, 12-13
Potato Latkes, Pearl's, 88
potato(es)
  Crescent Horns, 12-13
  Firecracker Potato Salad, 62
  Molly's Potato and Barley Soup, 26
  Pearl's Latkes, 88
  Roast Turkey with Carrots and, 82

pumpkin
  Acorn Squash Soup, 74
  Cookies, 77
  Pilgrim Pie, 84-85
  Pumpkin Cookies, 77
  Punch, Jack Frost's Tropical, 12

Q
Quiche, Quarterback, 15

R
Relish, Cranberry-Orange, 80
Rice Pilaf, Wild, 53

S
S'mores, September, 71
salad(s)
  All-American Fruit, 65
  Chopped Egg, 35
  Cucumber, Yogurt, and Mint, 52
  Easy Chicken, 69
  Firecracker Potato, 62
  Lucky Clover, 24
  Waldorf, 52
sauce(s)
  for Mrs. Claus's Plum Pudding,
    107
  Mushroom Gravy, 83
Seder Plate, 40-42
soup(s)
  Acorn Squash, 74
  Molly's Potato and Barley, 26
  Vegetarian Matzoh Ball, 43
Stars and Stripes Fusilli, 63
Strawberries, Chocolate-Dipped, 49
Stuffing, Chestnut, 81
Sufganiyot/Jelly Doughnuts, Uncle
    Solly's, 90-91
Sunday Roast Lamb, 37
Sweet and Sour Meatballs, 54
Sweet Potato Pudding, 95

T

Three-Bean Chili and Guacamole, 14

Turkey with Potatoes and Carrots, 82

V

Vegetable Kebabs, Veteran's, 55

vegetarian dishes
  Black-Eyed Pea Cutlets, 97
  Matzoh Ball Soup, 43
  Vegetable Kebabs, 55
  Virtual Burgers, 70

Vegetarian Matzoh Ball Soup, 43

Virtual Burgers, 70

W

Waffles, Belgian, 58

Waldorf Salad, 52

Wild Rice Pilaf, 53